ON BENDED KNEES

KNEES

ON BENDED KNEES

MARTIN GOODMAN

BARBICAN PRESS

This paperback edition published by Barbican Press:
London and Los Angeles

Copyright © Martin Goodman, 2022

First published by Macmillan, London, 1992

Registered office: 1 Ashenden Road, London E5 0DP

www.barbicanpress.com

@barbicanpress1

Cover by Rawshock Design

Cover photo: EAST GERMANY. Berlin. 1975. Boy in a Backyard Sophienstraße Berlin-Mitte. Thomas Hoepker/Magnum Photos

A CIP catalogue for this book is available from the British Library

ISBN: 978-1-909954-50-2

Typeset in Adobe Garamond

Typeset by Imprint Digital Ltd

Praise for Martin Goodman's *On Bended Knees*

Shortlisted for the Whitbread First Novel Prize

A perceptive, moving novel. Martin Goodman takes fierce delight in cutting through the easy clichés about the 'new' Europe.

~ Christopher Hope

Goodman's quirky first novel heralds a new dawn for British writing.
~ Malcolm Handley, *Daily Post*

This excellent first novel's central character is so completely realised he could have walked out of one of those enigmatic Bruce Chatwin pieces about old mysterious European types. Its basic, simplistic construction combines notions of guilt, memory, family and love into a book that's built to last long after the sell-by date of most first novels. I would be surprised if this didn't turn out to be one of the most promising debuts of the year.
~ David Darby, *Time Out*

A first novel of deceptive simplicity, which casts an absorbed and occasion-ally chilling eye over the complexities of family life, national identity and the horrors of recent European history.

~ D.J. Taylor

On Bended Knees is puzzling at first, because Tomas, who wants to tell his own story with proper attention – 'on bended knees' – seems to have very little personality, or even particular preference. But you come to see that he is conserving himself deliberately against the old suffering, the tired old guilt of the adults. He is biding his time. DJ Taylor has called *On Bended Knees* "deceptively simple", but I can't see what's deceptive about it. Simplicity is a great virtue, in novels as elsewhere. After all, it can only be produced from sincerity.

~ Penelope Fitzgerald, *The Evening Standard*

Goodman's quirkily charming novel interweaves a young man's search for selfhood in provincial Britain with the mysteries of his mother's German past.
~ Natasha Walker, *Vogue*

The novel's blunt, no-frills economy is part of its charm. Goodman writes with flare and panache, and the narrative fizzes along. Goodman's novel soars.

~ Michael Wright, *The Times*

A professional combination of rite-of-passage novel and cultural quest. The troubled half-German adolescent hero, Tomas, goes to stay with relatives in Berlin, following the disturbing death of his father. That city is brilliantly seen through the hero's eyes, as is the character who effectively steals the novel, the blind and autocratic Herr Poppel. The novel comes most to life when Tomas and Poppel are taking their walks around the divided city's streets and parks, the older man dispensing the secrets of longevity, the younger man hesitantly challenging him on the implications of his cast-iron pronouncements and their relation to Germany's guilty past. A very impressive debut.

~ Colin Donald, *The Scotsman*

'This quiet and subtle study of reconciliation tends to stick with English understatement and eschew German grandeur. No matter, Britain has squads of youngish writers trained to squeeze the last drop of moral juice out of the Second World War and its aftermath. It takes a braver soul, like Goodman, to hint that postwar babes should try instead to lay these ghosts to rest.

~ Boyd Tomkin, *The Observer*

Martin Goodman's award winning roster of books, both fiction and nonfiction, draw on his work and travels around the globe. He is Emeritus Professor of Creative Writing at the University of Hull, and has degrees from Leeds University, and a PhD in Creative Writing from Lancaster University. He lives with his husband, James Thornton, between London, Suffolk, Los Angeles and the South of France.

'Such narrow, narrow confines we live in. Every so often, one of us primates escapes these dimensions, as Martin Goodman did. All we can do is rattle the bars and look after him as he runs into the hills. We wait for his letters home.' ~ *The Los Angeles Times*

Martingoodman.com

@MartinGoodman2

Also by Martin Goodman

Novels

J SS Bach
Forever Konrad
Slippery When Wet
Look Who's Watching
I Was Carlos Castaneda

Nonfiction

Client Earth
Suffer & Survive: The Extreme Life of J.S. Haldane
On Sacred Mountains
In Search of the Divine Mother

For my sisters, Michelle & Elizabeth

Preface to the 30th Anniversary Edition

In London in the late 1980s one literary agent stood out. I learned that by checking who represented writers that shaped me: Bruce Chatwin, Ian McEwan, A.S. Byatt, Peter Carey, Kazuo Ishiguro, Anita Desai, J.G. Farrell, Thomas Kenneally, Angela Carter, Bernard McLaverty. Deborah Rogers took care of them all.

Salman Rushdie had just heaved himself out of Deborah's care. Bruce Chatwin too. Caryl Phillips took breaks from an Arvon Foundation writing retreat we shared to make loud calls from the payphone in the lobby. He too was quitting Deborah. I figured she had a vacancy. With my manuscript in a plastic bag I set off for her mews office in Portobello.

Even then you didn't turn up to see agents unannounced. 'Have you an appointment?' the young receptionist asked.

No, I said, and smiled, but I had come down from Glasgow for the day. This was all I'd come for. I didn't mind waiting. I could wait as long as it took.

The receptionist made a call. I was allowed to wait. Deborah wore a bright red suit. Her posture was one of someone who peered. She stared at me from under her blond fringe and gave me a little lecture. Writers can't simply show up like this. And then she opened the door and invited me into her office.

'Take a seat,' she started to say, and then realized they were all taken. Each seat was filled with a pile of books. More books spilled across the surface of her desk. Stacks of them covered the carpet where others had toppled. She cleared space and we settled down to talk.

We spoke first about why I had chosen to bring my work to her. And then about my life, my writing, and the novel that was in my bag. It was set in a dystopian London in which no girls had been born for sixteen years. This was not really Deborah's thing. She opened the ringbinder and studied the opening pages. Something in the voice attracted her.

'I'm really busy,' she said. 'A new agent would be able to give you much more time than I will. Are you sure you want me?'

'Absolutely sure,' I said.

And Deborah tried. She sent out the book (published many years later in a wholly different version as *Ectopia*) and publishers returned it.

Deborah was more precious to me than that book. 'Stop sending it out,' I told her. 'I'll write you a novel you *can* sell.'

The one I had in mind was about a boy who went to a divided Berlin and, by becoming a rabbit and burrowing under the Berlin wall, he reconciled East and West. But since an editor at Bloomsbury had turned down my previous novel for being 'too remarkable', I wrote this book without the fantasy rabbit. It became *On Bended Knees*.

The phone rang in my tenement flat. It was Martin Fletcher from Picador. He had only kind things to say. (Or maybe that's my fond memory. When we sat down to edit, he asked me to cut the original second chapter.) Deborah had sold my first novel.

That was thirty years ago, and the question that drove me then still drives me. How are the effects of war passed down through succeeding generations?

In 1975 I was selected on a program that placed British school leavers in West Berlin. My job was in a department store. My home was a room in a large and somewhat Gothic house belonging to the Popendicker family. Herr Popendicker was an ex-Nazi on the War Crimes Register. He was in his seventies, his wife in her early forties, and they had a teenage son and daughter; the girl was lively, the boy hid behind his curtain of long hair.

On my first meeting with Herr Popendicker he lectured me about the authorship of Shakespeare's works, his favoured candidate being Queen Elizabeth I. Knowing more of my culture than I of his, he enjoyed challenging me on my own turf. And by inviting me into his family home, onto *his* own turf, he was relinking our two cultures in some way.

My father, an electro plater, spent the war working for the aeroplane manufacturer Vickers Armstrong. They provided the fleet of Wellington Bombers that dominated the Royal Air Force's early offensive missions in WW2. On 25th August 1940 these bombers took part in the first night-time raid on Berlin. One night two years later, 1000 RAF aircraft dropped 1455 tons of explosive on the city of Cologne. More than half of these planes were Wellington Bombers. Most of the bombs were incendiaries, designed to provoke overwhelming fires. 45,000 citizens were made homeless, and 465 killed. The city centre was turned to ruin.

To the British this air raid was one strike in a march toward victory. By coming to Berlin I'd walked into a different narrative. Victories for one side meant horrors for the other. The teenage me and the septuagenarian Popendicker shared beers in the evening and the divide between us shrank a little. Sheepishly, he told me how he had captained the platoon which shot down the first Wellington Bomber over German soil.

Frau Popendicker let me into another aspect of her husband's history. Though much taller than his wife, at the beginning of their relationship she had been able to carry him in her arms. He was fresh from a prisoner of war camp in the Soviet Union, weighing 60lbs.

He admitted when I challenged him that much of what the Nazis did was deplorable. But he spoke as if the Nazi program had simply gone astray from its initial intent to restore order to the nation. As an example, he told how wire was commonly strung across roads to decapitate drivers and their passengers in open top cars. That, he explained, was stopped by the Nazis. Did he expect me to weigh this in the balance against the Final Solution? Popendicker felt stuck in West Berlin, for any train ride out of the city would lead him through East Germany. When East German guards checked his name against the War Crimes Register he feared they would haul him away.

Herr Popendicker held fondly to his past. He once brought a treasure to our drinking sessions and gifted it to me. It was a coloured souvenir postcard of Hitler's mountain retreat in Berchtesgaden. When he retired from teaching classics Popendicker took up the study of medicine with the goal of prolonging life. He would go on to buy a sanatorium in the Black Forest and offer me a free series of injections. I declined.

A colleague at work in the department store, who looked like an old man to me, took a few weeks to break his silence. The last Englishman he saw had been his wartime enemy. 'What do you think of Churchill?' he asked. He pronounced each /ch/ of the name softly, like a /sh/. 'Shurshill' he said, and I couldn't understand him at first. I told him Churchill was a strong leader, but remembered the old man I'd seen wheeled to his window on his birthday. The TV screen showed the streets outside packed with cheering crowds.

'Who's that?' I asked. 'Churchill,' my mother answered. 'The most important man in Britain.'

A frequent landscape of my dreams has been the blasted shells of German buildings and rubble. Such shells and rubble still dominated the outskirts of 1970s Dresden. There I met an old woman who sat in a room surrounded by photographs of her son in his military uniform. He was probably eighteen in the photograph, like I was then. He had been killed in the war. Her city had been burnt to the ground. She could not bring herself to speak to me.

The same war consumed my mother's childhood. In the 1960s the city of Leicester was still too exhausted to deal with its ruins. Bomb damage had ripped away the facades of buildings, like you could do with a doll's house wall. I could look through to an upstairs bedroom and see striped wallpaper on display to the world, and a mirror hanging askew from its chain. My schoolteachers were war veterans. One was kind and another mean. 'He's psychologically damaged by the war,' my mother explained, 'and that's what you have to understand. Be glad you didn't have to go through the war. Whatever a teacher does to you in a classroom really isn't so bad.'

1970s Berlin was divided into sectors. The British, American and French sectors constituted West Berlin. A short walk from my home and I could touch the city's surrounding wall. The Russian sector had become East Berlin. Berlin was torn between East and West, communism and capitalism, both sides still shell-shocked by war.

I was in Germany, in the countryside near Limburg, when the galleys for *On Bended Knees* came through. It was 1991. I managed a lightning return to Berlin to fact check and map my memory against reality. The city's parallel ring of walls, the space between them once filled with landmines and coils of barbed wire, had been replaced by bulldozed wasteland. The Berlin wall had fallen. The city felt dazed, its fractured elements waiting to reconnect.

In 2002 I was teaching a class of sixteen and seventeen year-olds in an English college. They knew nothing of the Iron Curtain, of the Berlin wall, of the Cold War, or that Europe had been riven by an ideological divide. The adults around them weren't conditioned by growing up in a world war.

And now another twenty years have passed. For me, *On Bended Knees* becomes more poignant. Wars are deeply scarring. Refugees now stream from climate change as well as global wars because their home lives are too dangerous to bear. It takes conscious effort to keep our local worlds safe. Not too long ago, on the fringes of living memory, even in Europe we tore each other apart.

This is a human story from an earlier time. Let it help us remember.

Martin Goodman – December 2021

Some words for Gran, before you start

Gran could have settled her bones into the leatherette upholstery of Grandpa's Rover. Instead she sat rigid on the bench-like seat of a bus, her head turned to stare into the window. There she found a reflection of herself, one which scrubbed her face clean of age. In what was left she could recognise herself in middle age, herself as a young woman, as a little girl.

It gave her something to do. There wasn't much to distract her on the bus route to Coventry. The sky was blank with cloud, the landscape of low grey buildings and dusty fields untouched by imagination.

'The last I saw of Coventry was its orange glow as the city burned to the ground,' Gran had said as we waited at the bus station, blowing out clouds of breath like the buses' exhaust fumes. 'We could see it even from here.'

The bus was slower than a car, more uncomfortable. Every mile of this journey would be made to count. Years later, when I first went to Rome, I found a building that housed a long run of stone steps leading to a high altar. The steps were rounded and smooth, worn away by centuries of pilgrims who had climbed each one on their knees. Gran would no doubt have gone down on her knees and joined them. I ran up and down the alternative steps to the side.

Old folks sit and think a lot. Perhaps it's because of the aches whenever they move, their bones and muscles grinding as they creak through the final years. To sit still and escape into the past must be a huge relief.

Me, I'm still young. I'm happy to run. You have to wrap a seat belt around me to keep me still.

Gran and Grandpa and Mum and Dad and everyone I've met along the way have put everything into my head. My life's made up of all of their stories. It's time to tell my own.

There's a time to run, and a time to go on your knees.

Wake up, Gran. Make room for me. I'm getting down on my knees to join you.

Part One

ENGLAND
1963 – 1966

One

A two-bar electric fire had been scorching the air in their bedroom for days and nights. Some of its heat leaked under the door to where I stood on the landing.

'Mum,' I called softly, to let her know I was back from school.

She slid her body into the space as I pushed open the door. 'Hello,' she mouthed.

Dad's head was tipped back on his bank of pillows to stare at the glass bowl of light in the ceiling, his mouth open and lit grey.

'He's all right,' Mum said. 'He's all right, Tomas. Don't be frightened. He won't do anything. It's out of our hands now.' She gripped my shoulder and pulled me into the room.

'Sit with him, Tomas. I'm going for help.'

In a quick shuffle of her grey slippers she was round me, through the door and out on to the landing, pulling the door closed behind her. The stairs rumbled and the front door slammed as she left the house. The Yale lock was on. She had locked herself out. She never had a key in those days. Times I got home from school and found her sitting on the front door step.

'It's your father,' she would explain. 'He's not well enough to come to the door,' and she waited for me to let us both in.

I moved along the side of the bed and eased myself down, taking care not to tip Dad towards me. His hands lay palm upward on top of the bedclothes, their fingers slightly curled. I took hold of one and folded his fingers closer round mine.

'Mum's gone,' I said.

It was strange to talk. Words sounded thin and were left to float around the room looking for company.

'I've just got back from school. We played football this afternoon. My team won.'

I was seven. I had just started playing football. I had been picked second from last. We had won five-two. The two goals had been let in while I was in goal. There wasn't much else to say about school. As I sat on my stool in a science lesson and gazed at a squirrel playing between the trees outside, a length of rubber pipe was thwacked across my thigh to remind me where I was. It left a red mark that I could still see when I changed for games.

But Dad didn't want to know that.

'It's hot in here, Dad. Do you want me to open a window?'

Sweat dripped down my sides under my school shirt. Beyond the window the sky showed the clear blue of autumn, but thick burgundy curtains were drawn to suck up its light.

Dad's hand stayed closed around my own, but I thought I heard him speak. It was a sputtering in the back of his throat, like the fast ticking of the bedside clock. I couldn't make it out. I leaned forward and listened as juices gurgled up into his mouth. Grey bristles of a new moustache furred the space above his lips, and a beard like mould shaded his jowl. The tongue had shrivelled to a dry flap, its point moving slowly like a tortoise's head. A puff of stale air gusted out from where the grey of the mouth got lost in darkness. Then the view was sealed off, the mouth shut, the lips stuck together for the final word to build up inside.

'Ma,' Dad said.

'Mum will be back soon. She's only gone to phone for help.' His eyes stared at the lightbulb and his jaw sagged. 'She loves you, Dad. We love you. I love you.'

I held on to the hand. The fingertips turned cold as I spoke, a cold that inched over the knuckles and spread across the palm.

'You're cold, Dad.' But the room was so hot. 'You're turning really cold.'

The fingers lost the colour of flesh and turned blue.

There was a hammering on the door and the shouts of Mum, but I couldn't go. The hammering stopped as the sound of an ambulance's bell swelled down the street. Feet stamped through the sudden silence, down the passageway to the unlocked back door.

Mum pushed open the bedroom door, though an ambulance-man was first into the room. He prised my hand free and picked up Dad's wrist. Turning to Mum he shook his head.

She raced inside and pulled me away like she was rescuing me from a fire. Kneeling down she took hold of my arms and shook them to make my body tremble.

'Go downstairs with Maureen. I'll be down in a minute.'

Mrs Maureen Colleen was standing on the landing. She picked me up from behind and swung me round, linking her hands underneath my backside. I had to curl my legs around her back and hold on fast around her neck as she carried me downstairs.

'It's a shock,' she announced.

She had settled us both in a chair and pressed my head against her breasts where she could stroke it.

'A shock, but not to worry. The man has no troubles now. Your father's with his maker and all is well. Don't struggle. Don't strain yourself. The tears will come in their own sweet time, and then you can smile again. Now tell me, Tomas, did your father have anything to say? Did he have any last words?'

She let me climb off her lap and stand up.

'Did he have any words of comfort?'

'He just said Ma.'

Mum came in as I spoke.

'Did you hear that, Margaret?' Maureen Colleen's cheeks puffed tight and rosy and her mouth squinted a smile. 'Your name was on his lips. With his dying breath Douglas spoke your name.'

'I heard the boy.' Mum stepped round, knelt in front of me again and placed her hands on my shoulders, but turned to face her friend. 'My name's not Ma. Ma can mean many things. Mother, Martha, Marlene, Mark. Maybe he wanted some marmalade. He was that stupid at times.'

'Ma is Margaret,' Maureen insisted. 'Don't question it. It's a miracle he got a sound out at all. A miracle, Margaret, so think yourself blessed. Blessed for the devotion you've shown. The chance to pass away peacefully in his own home was all he asked. With God's help and yours that's what's been granted. He's at peace, Margaret. Now you be at peace.'

One ambulanceman looked in through the front door as another left the house. 'Sorry we can't take him for you, love. Only this isn't an emergency proper, and we're on call. Give your doctor a bell. He'll know what to do.'

Maureen stood up. 'I'll ring him for you. It's no bother. You two wait here. I'll be back in a while and brew us some tea.'

'Don't close the door,' Mum called after her as she left the room.

'Well,' she sighed when we were alone, and she reached forward to pinch my cheek. I watched the shock drift from her face as she smiled the words that were left unsaid. Then she collapsed back into the cushions of the armchair.

'You were with him then, Tomas,' she said. 'He had you with him at the end. I suppose it's as well.'

'Is he still upstairs?'

'Don't worry. He won't move. Not on his own. The doctor will come, then the undertaker. He'll be carried away after that. Dying in peace is fine for the dead, Tomas. For the dead, everything is easy. For the living, that's when the trouble begins.'

She caught my eye and patted her lap. I turned and looked away from her, through the window and up into the blue of the sky. We could open the curtains in Dad's room now. Perhaps I should go upstairs and do it. Dad liked to look into the sky.

'Tomas, come here!'

Mum's voice was on the crest of a sob. I turned back and saw her hold out her hands, her face twisted to free the flow of tears. It was the power of sorrow. I ran towards it and climbed on to her lap, holding her tight to absorb the shock of her weeping.

Two

'You didn't have to go to school today,' Mum said. 'No one expected it. You must have crept out. I would have stopped you if I'd heard.'

'You were asleep.'

The bedroom door had been open, the window pushed up and the curtains drawn back. Light filled the room but it looked empty. The mattress was on the floor and Mum's head on the pillow, with the eiderdown pulled close to her chin. The lines that creased her face by day were smoothed away and her hair floated high like a snapshot taken in the wind.

'Sleep!' she said. 'I chased it round all night but it didn't come till dawn. I'd sooner die myself than pass another night like that.'

She dried her hands on her apron and untied its bow. Once it had been covered with a pattern of bright forget-me-nots, but white clouds of age and use had been worn into the material. She lifted its band of string over her neck and dumped the apron into the kitchen bin.

'Everything looks so grubby today,' she said.

'Mr Filey came into the class this morning. He said I needed a haircut.'

'Mr Filey is bald. A man with no hair will always be jealous of you, my darling. Your brown locks are too beautiful.' She brushed her hand across my forehead. 'I'll write him a letter. You take it with you tomorrow. The man's a headmaster. We can't expect him to be sensitive but we can educate him a little. Did you tell him about your father?'

'No.'

'Then he has no excuse. Your hair is perfect for school. A funeral is a different matter. We'll get along to see Mr MacGregor before he shuts.'

Mum patted me on the back of the head and sent me to sit on a chair at the back of the room while she spoke with the barber, Mr MacGregor. Normally she just instructed a light trim then left to do her shopping, but today she had more to explain. The voices were low and hidden beneath the sound of the radio playing from its shelf in the corner. As she finished, the man in the chair between them turned to look at me.

The barber turned too. His eyes were round, like tiny glass marbles that were black at the heart. With a finger he lifted a corner of his thick black moustache to show me a smile.

Mum dropped her fingers against the palm of her hand in a wave. The bell above the door rang as it opened to let her out. I watched through the slats of the venetian blind as she marched past.

I liked looking out through the window. Men who left after their haircuts would face their reflections in the plate glass and scrub their hair with their hands, pulling a funny face when they noticed me looking at them. They were adjusting to life on the street. Inside it was a kinder world. They sat in silence with *Titbits*, *The Weekly* News or a car magazine, or joined in the banter about cars, fishing, football and escaping the wife.

It was my club. I picked up a copy of *Buster* from a rack of comics and sat back to wait my turn.

When it came, a smaller platform was inserted for me between the arms of the chair manned by Mr MacGregor. He swirled round a cloak and tied it around my neck. Some pumps of a pedal raised me closer to tubs of Brylcreem, combs tied to a card, boxes of razor blades and condoms, all spilled out along a glass shelf as though not for sale. My glasses were taken off and the scene in the mirror was blurred. The barber's hands rested on my shoulders.

'What can we do for you today, Master Christie?'

'Just a trim, please.' It was the standard question and response, as though the choice were mine.

Mr MacGregor began to comb my hair.

'You'll leave here a smart young man,' he said, then paused. He was studying me in the mirror. 'Your dad was nearly blind without his glasses. I sometimes thought his eyes had more important things to do than seeing. They were wonderful, your dad's eyes. Brown and deep and swimming with life. You've got the same eyes, you and him.'

I thought of the eyes that stared glazed and blind at the bedroom ceiling. Mr MacGregor began to snip around my head with his scissors.

'Your head's like his. It's funny, cutting a boy's hair as well as his father's. You get to see the resemblances. He was proud of you. He came in here the day you got accepted to the grammar school. Said it was proof there were brains in your family. I told him, you've got the same head, you and your kid. There's the same brains at work. He was one of the brightest men I knew, your dad. It didn't matter that he was just a postman. It even seemed right somehow, him carrying all those words around in his bag. He was the only postman I ever heard of who would go back after his round and help people write their replies.'

He moved around to stand between me and the mirror and lifted my fringe with his comb.

'You're the image of him, you know that? His face was long like yours. He had those cheekbones. You'll have his build too. Always lean, he was. Never an ounce of fat on him. Always looked so fit, he did.'

I thought of the sunken cheeks and the withered body laid out in the bed.

'Don't you ever forget your dad, Tomas. Keep a picture of him in your head. You'll find nothing better to live up to in this life. Turn out like your dad and you won't have gone far wrong.'

The scissors started to snip. My hair fell on to his apron and down to the ground. An older boy in a blue nylon coat bent his head over a broom and swept it up, dropping it into a hessian sack. It would be used for stuffing cushion or making wigs.

Dad would have needed one of those wigs. He hadn't been to the barber's for a while. His hair fell out on its own.

Three

The headmaster had his own way of entering the room. He turned the handle sharply so we would all hear it snap in its frame. It was a signal for the whole class. Our chairs grated across the cement floor as we shoved them back with bare legs, abandoning the lesson to rise to our feet behind our individual desks. He took the sound as his cue to push at the door and enter.

'Good morning, Mr Filey sir.'

'Good morning, boys.'

He stood in the doorway and surveyed us before giving the command to sit, then walked over to take the register from the teacher. The unusual thickness told him of the letter inside. He took it out and flapped it in front of us.

'Who can this be from?'

I raised my hand.

'To the front, Christie!'

I walked forward to stand in front of him.

'Why, Christie, I must apologise. I didn't know you grew your hair so long for a reason. You were hiding your ears. They are large, Christie. I must be careful what I say in future. You have ears like radar dishes. You must be able to hear everything I say. Turn and face the class, Christie.'

He crossed his arms to take hold of my ears and swivel me round.

'Never mind their laughter. This class is full of little boys. They're cruel by nature. They'll laugh at anything. The barber has played a joke on you and they think it's funny. So it is. You do look funny. You have spectacular ears, Christie. You will have to learn to live with them.'

He bent down to study me closer.

'Oh dear. I thought so. You're blushing, Christie. Your ears are turning pink. Pink is not a very manly colour. You must learn to bear your handicaps more bravely than this, my boy. Stand there and practise while I read this letter.'

He picked a pencil out of his jacket pocket, slit the envelope open, and took out the sheet of paper. I turned to watch him read it. For a moment his eyebrows arched clear of his round spectacle frames, then a scowl brought them back down.

'Christie, go and wait outside my room.'

A headmaster is an expert on schooling. I see that now. I can look back and picture the man's face at the window of his office. He stares out across the playground where the most ineffectual teacher has been set on duty. Games turn into fights, friends link into gangs, and schoolboys' heads are toughened against concrete. This is a preparatory school.

The man prepares the children in his charge for the life he has known. He was too tender when he was sent to war. The same won't happen to his schoolboys. He presides over their education and doesn't see a playground. He sees a battlefield.

The headmaster's room was a large stock cupboard, its walls padded with books stacked on steel racks from floor to ceiling. His desk stood beneath the single square window, which looked out over the school yard. On a nail to one side of the window hung a gas mask, and from a nail on the other side the black plimsoll that was used for beatings.

This was the bonery. Stories told how sometimes boys were so bad that a beating was not enough. When the punishment was complete their bones were stored under the floorboards.

I waited in the corridor in the way we had been taught, with my hands clasped behind my back and my nose touching the wall. The headmaster arrived, opened the door, and walked inside.

'Come in,' he called.

Mr Filey's round head was silhouetted against the window. What hair he had was sleeked with oil around the clean bald dome of his head. It was as round as a balloon, but had the two prim buttons of his ears instead of a balloon's normal one. My memory pumps the whole man full of wind till he expands to the size of a barrage balloon. Such a man can swell till he blocks out the sun. I checked and saw the plimsoll was still on its nail.

'Were you born in a barn, boy?'

I walked back to shut the door.

'Now sit down. We've got some talking to do.'

The chair was set across the desk from the headmaster's own. I tucked my feet behind the wooden bar that joined its front legs.

'Your letter has news,' he said, while studying it. It was unfolded to lie flat on his desk. Suddenly he lifted his head and stared at me through his spectacles. 'Your father is dead.'

He watched for a reaction. I sat still.

'You know that, of course. You knew it. Perhaps the whole school knew it. I understand he died two days ago. Was I the only one who didn't know? I do my best, I eat my carrots like every good boy should, but it is no use. I still cannot see when I am left in the dark. I don't like being left in the dark, Christie. Why couldn't you tell me the news yourself? Why leave it to your poor mother?'

I stared back at him, still silent.

'Well?'

'I don't know, sir.'

'Rubbish, Christie. You know everything. You're a know-all. Do you think that's good, Christie, being a little know-it-all?'

'No, sir.'

'Well, you're wrong. Know-alls are fine. Only most of them make one big mistake. They hold everything back. They don't share what they know. You're bright, Christie. Very bright. So tell me the answer to this question. What use is a leader who sneaks off when no one is looking?'

'No use sir.'

'Neither to himself, nor to anyone else. We're born to serve, and the man who leads is the greatest servant of all. Your father's dead and you're seven years old. That's too young. This death could poison you. We've got to get it out of your system. Do you know what it means, your father's death?'

'He's gone to heaven.'

'That's what it means to him. What does it mean to you?'

'I don't know, sir.'

'It means you're responsible. There's just your mother and you now, so you're responsible for everything. Your father's gone. He's dead. It's a hard fact to swallow but you'll never do it with a lump in your throat.'

'I didn't do it, sir.'

'Didn't do what? Didn't let me know yourself that your father had died? That's nothing. There's something much more important that you didn't do. What do you think that is?'

'I didn't kill my father.'

'Of course you didn't. But he's dead all the same. How do you feel about that?'

I blinked back at him.

'You know the stories about my room? Do you know why it's called the bonery?'

He crossed to a large steel cupboard by the side wall and pulled the door wide open. Books were stacked on shelves set back on the inside, but a clatter of noise came from the inside of the door itself. The knotted limbs of a small white skeleton were swinging against the metal.

'This,' the head announced, chucking the skeleton under its chin, 'is a boy who didn't do what he had to do. He refused to grow up. Is this what you want to be like?'

He let the skeleton hang as evidence for a moment then slammed it back into darkness. He leaned back against the cupboard and watched me, then took a white handkerchief out of his pocket. Sticking his index finger up through the centre he made the first of three knots and soon he had a puppet draped over his hand. It danced slowly at first, a tiny and tentative ghost, then floated down to pinch my nose between its sleeves.

'Blow,' he said.

I swiped the handkerchief away.

'What's the matter, Christie?' the headmaster whined. 'Won't you let me blow your nose? Do you want your daddy to do it for you?'

'Dad's dead!' I shouted. The words took up all the breath I had so I sobbed for more.

'Your daddy's dead, you say?' He stood back to mime his horror, but I looked away. He knelt down instead and laid his hands on my shoulders. 'That's right, Christie,' he assured me, his voice cold now. 'Your dad's dead.'

Pulling me off my chair and towards him so swiftly that my legs buckled, he gathered me into his arms and reached up a hand to stroke my head.

'Your dad's dead.' Tears were beginning to gather behind his voice. 'So you cry, my boy. Cry for all you're worth.'

I made my body stiff and pushed one of my shoulders into the man's chest to break free. Mr Filey stiffened too. He stood up and moved back round to the far side of his desk.

'Sit on the chair,' he instructed, 'while I write a reply to your mother.'

His hand was sweaty as he gripped the pen. He wiped the palm on his trouser leg before bending in concentration over the paper. The letter took barely five minutes to compose. He blotted it dry and sealed it in an envelope.

'Give this to your mother after school.' He held it out so that I had to climb down from my chair to fetch it. 'She'll explain what it's about. Now hurry back to your class. You've got a lot to learn.'

Four

Mum walked into the playground to meet me. As I held out the envelope she held out a plastic bag folded to about the same size.

She gave in first and took the letter.

'This is from Mr Filey? He was good to you today, yes?' She waved the letter so it trembled in her hand in a mini show of triumph, then slid it into her coat pocket.

She handed me the bag. Wrapped in a paper bag inside was a thin black tie made of a funny material that stretched when pulled.

'It's for the funeral,' she explained. 'It's like a medal. You wear it so people will know you as a brave young man. A brave but scruffy young man. What have you got in those pockets?'

She patted one of my jacket pockets and reached inside.

'Chestnuts,' she announced, picking one out.

'Conkers,' I corrected her.

'Why so many? Nobody needs so many. They're pulling your jacket out of shape. Throw them away.'

'I can't. The other boys gave them to me.' They had come up to me during the dinner hour, a whole procession of them, and each given me a conker from their collections.

'Your father dies and they give you... conkers.' She tried out the word and liked it. It was earthy. 'Is this a tradition?'

'It's a game. Two people play. You both hang a conker on a bit of string and take it in turns to smash at the other one.'

'And who wins?'

'The one that doesn't get smashed.'

She nodded her head.

'I understand,' she conceded. 'It's a sensible game. It holds no illusions. But they will ruin your jacket nevertheless. Put the tie in your pocket. The conkers can go in the plastic bag, and the bag in the satchel.'

Mum enjoyed fitting things into a system.

We were the last people in the playground. Some of the other mothers had turned to glance at Mum as they passed. She had not yet got to know them. They chatted to each other but simply nodded their heads at Mum. She nodded back if she saw them.

She folded her arms and tapped her foot in mock impatience as I transferred the conkers one by one into their bag.

'Ach, Junge Junge,' she said.

Her German was spoken like a sigh. I looked up at her and smiled. She dug her hands into my pockets to help, then bent down to fasten the satchel straps and hurry me along.

Taking each other by the hand we walked off home, the satchel thumping my leg with each big step.

'Read it to me,' she said, and handed the letter across the kitchen table.

My hand was sticky with the jam and butter from my sandwiches. Picking the letter up I started at the top, reading out the school's address, the date, and 'Dear Mrs Christie'.

She settled herself on the kitchen chair and tuned in.

Please accept my sincere condolences upon the death of your husband, and excuse my presumption in sending what must seem a bold letter at this delicate juncture.

I am pleased to think that the free place awarded to your son should allow his schooling to proceed without disruption. While Tomas has failings of hubris and concentration, the potential is there for him to do very well indeed.

In our interview this morning the boy expressed some emotion but immediately sought to suppress it and withdraw into his shell. I worry at the extent of personal loss this suggests in the death of his father, a loss that at his age might well be converted into a general sense of injustice.

Within my professional capacity as headmaster there are natural limits to the extent to which I can become directly involved with any one particular boy. However my experience has taught me the immense value to a boy of feeling a proper sense of trust in an older man. I would therefore take it as a privilege to be allowed to become that man, and to welcome him on a regular basis into my own home, where my wife might offer the practical comforts of a good tea from time to time. There are limits to the horizons a simple headmaster might spread before a boy, but I would be pleased to show him what I can.

I can only guess that such an offer might be welcome, but please don't hesitate to contact me should you wish to discuss any aspect of your son's future.

Yours sincerely,

Lewis Filey

'Well done,' Mum said, because the letter was so hard to read. She took it from me to help me with the pronunciation of the longer words before handing it back for me to read again.

'Well, what do you think?' she asked when I had finished.

'What does *hubris* mean?'

'Pride. *Stolz.*' She introduced all new words in both languages. 'It's Greek.'

'Mr Filey says I'm big-headed.'

'Then you must believe him, for Mr Filey is big-headed too. It's deep within his nature. Does he have any children of his own?'

'A daughter. Dorothy. I've seen her at the school a few times.'

'And how old is she?'

'About my age.'

'Good. Then she can be your friend. This world is full of father figures. Men who can't look after themselves love to look after others. But you go to an all-boys' school. A young girl for you to play with is not a bad thing. You can go home with Mr Filey and see how you like it.'

I carried my plate over to the sink and wiped my hands on the damp cloth that hung over the taps, then took the cloth back to wipe the red fingerprints of jam from the letter. As the cloth dragged across the paper the headmaster's tidy script collapsed into a pool of blue. Mum laughed at my alarm.

'Don't worry.' She screwed the letter up into a ball without staining her hands with its ink. 'They were only words. Words are never the truth. We don't have to save them.'

I stationed myself by the pedal bin and pressed down with my foot as the crumpled letter flew towards me. The lid rose and snapped closed to trap the letter inside.

'Good!' Mum clapped her hands and we both laughed. She slapped her knees and I jumped on to her lap.

'We are alive, Tomas.' She bounced me high so we could laugh into each other's faces. 'Alive! Alive! Alive!'

Five

Caterers were already installed in Gran's house when we arrived, arranging plates of sandwiches on the dining table. Cars lined the pavement outside, waiting to ferry us to the funeral.

Mum had accepted the arrangements without complaint. Gran's house was bigger and so more suitable, she agreed. She waited till Grandpa stood with his list by the front door, reading out who was to travel in which car, before she had her say.

'Tomas and I will travel alone,' she declared. 'In the rear car.'

There was no time for an argument. She reached past Grandpa to open the door and took hold of my hand. As we hurried out the first drops of rain splattered on to the concrete of the front path. The path was stained dark and shiny before we reached the gate.

We settled into the back seat of our chosen car. The others followed more carefully, bunched beneath umbrellas and casting looks at us before squashing themselves into the seats that were left.

Gran and Grandpa travelled in the car immediately in front of ours. The black feather in Gran's hat was crushed against the car's ceiling. Mum stared at it till the winking of the car's indicator light broke her from her thoughts. The fleet of cars was bearing the mourners through a green light and to the right. She leaned forward and struck the driver's shoulder with the knuckles of her fingers.

'Turn left,' she said.

'But...'

'Turn left, then follow the road till I say stop.'

He flicked up his indicator lever and wheeled the car round. Mum settled back in the comfort of the seat as we began to climb a hill. Away from the funeral cortege our crawling speed was out of place, but she seemed content.

The driver's hair was so short and fair that his skull shone through. Above his shirt collar was a band of white skin. There were blemishes of grime where the collar bent itself round. Mum said you could tell a man by his collar. She was staring at the collar now, passing judgement. Dad's were always immaculate when he went off on his round.

We climbed up the hill that led out of the town. Houses were set in ever larger gardens till the buildings disappeared and there was only countryside left. As the car passed over the brow of the hill a gentle panorama of further hills, stitched into fields and laced with hedges, rolled out before us.

The car pulled off the road on to a grass verge. Mum accepted the move without complaint, opened her car door and stepped out, reaching back a hand to guide me out on to the road beside her. Hand in hand we walked to the front of the car, where she lifted me up and set my feet down on the bonnet, curving one hand around my waist to give me support.

She turned back to the view. 'Do you see that? That's the earth you see out there. That's the body of the world. When we bury your father, this is what we're doing. We are adding him to the earth.'

And the earth was also ashes and fire and fumes and the sounds of savage wild weeping. She knew that then though I only learned it later. That was why she shuddered.

'Come,' she said when we had both got soaked. Through the windscreen I saw the driver watching us, his face going blurred then clear as the wipers swept from side to side.

We trod through mud and wet grass towards the passenger door.

'We'll sit in the front,' Mum announced, having already settled me near the handbrake. She climbed in herself and closed the door. 'It's too big in the back. Like an empty ballroom. And Tomas never gets the chance to travel by car. His father didn't drive.'

She had picked the driver's hat up from the seat and was holding it on her lap, spinning it slowly round as she fingered its rim.

'Put that in the back,' he ordered.

She twisted round and dropped the hat on the seat behind her, as though she followed orders every day.

'We're going back to the church,' he told her.

'Of course.' She waited until the car was turned round before speaking again. 'Please do me a favour. Explain this car to the boy. What the bits of a car are called and what they do. I don't even know the words.'

He glanced at her a moment then moved up the gears in silence.

'The heater would be a good place to start,' she persisted. 'Which button do you have to press?'

He pushed a switch, drew down a knob, and fans whirred to blow warm air around our legs.

'And what's this?' she asked, pointing.

'The choke.'

'What does it do?'

'You pull it out when the engine's cold.'

'And this?'

'The gear lever.'

'And what happens with that?'

He sighed before starting to explain. She interrupted him.

'It's not for me. I have no interest, but the boy needs to know. You're a good man. You tell him.'

I studied the controls and asked my questions till we had drawn up outside the church.

Mum's suit was the colour of ashes, grey and woollen and pulling at her knees as she strode up the path through the churchyard. I stumbled along beside her with my hand clamped in hers.

'They can burn me!' She turned her head to spin her shout into the poplar trees that lined the graveyard. 'When I go they must burn me. Burn me and throw my ashes in the bin. You remember that, Tomas.'

She stopped and let go of my hand to grip me by the shoulders. She didn't shake me, but the trembling in her hands passed down my spine.

'If you still care enough when I am dead, have me burnt!'

I looked up at her. Muscles were working in her cheeks that I never knew she had. The rain pressed her hair flat and washed down her face. She lifted her chin away from me and stared through the rain up into the sky.

'God!' she cried. 'We don't need all this!'

Her right hand waved a tired circle in the air, taking in the church and the churchyard to return them all to God, then she let it fall. Her arms hung by her side.

I waited for the thunder of response, but the day was too sullen to find voice. From inside the church I could hear the organist trilling out high notes against some heavy chords, killing time till the service could start. Grandpa was in the church porch. He opened an umbrella then stepped out to splash his way towards us, giving me a quick smile before reaching out to touch Mum's shoulder.

'Margaret,' he said. 'Come inside. You'll catch your deaths out here.'

She looked up at the dark circle of the umbrella that sheltered her from the sky, then slowly turned till she was facing the man.

'You're drenched,' he said. 'Haven't you got coats?'

'We dressed for a funeral. Not for the weather.'

'But look at poor Tom.'

'He's not poor Tom.' She brought me round to stand between her and her father-in-law and placed a hand on my shoulder. 'He's brave Tomas.'

Grandpa smiled. He held his umbrella to one side to shelter her and she let herself be led towards the church.

A crowd of faces turned to us. They were impatient of waiting but tried not to show it. We overtook Grandpa and hurried down the aisle. When we reached the pine coffin, set on its trestles higher than my head, Mum shuffled quickly along the vacant pew. She released her hold on me so she could cover her face with her hands. Her shivers were so violent her knees cracked against the ledge for hymn books in front of her. Those around pulled back at the noise. I reached up to pull hard on her wet sleeve.

'Test me,' Mum said, days afterwards. She had sworn she could remember every single detail about the day.

'What was Gran carrying?'

'Oh, that's too easy. A rose. A single red rose pressed splendidly against the black fur of her coat.'

'How many wreaths were there?'

'Three. Three too many. I asked that there should be none, but your Gran does things her own way. Hers was enormous and gaudy. It's lucky your dad was dead. So many flowers pressed down on him like that would have done his asthma no good at all.'

'What music did they play?'

'By the grave, you mean?'

I nodded.

'The Posthorn Gallop. On two trumpets. You'd think with so many postmen gathered around they could have found an actual posthorn. And the second trumpeter, the one who pointed his instrument down at your father's coffin as though trying to wake him up, had a fingernail black with dried blood. It was his index finger. He must have trapped it. Whenever he had to press it down on its brass button his left eyebrow jumped a little with the pain. So you see? I do remember everything. Now it's your turn. What do you remember best?'

Gran had stood still in the stone porch as the coffin was carried out and into the storm, as though she had launched it. She watched the rain bounce against its lid, then turned to lean forward and grab me by the shoulder. If I had stepped back she would have fallen flat on her face. Her eyes were ringed with dark circles.

'He's in you,' she announced, and the fingers of her hand bit into the muscles around my shoulder blade as though to make sure. Her voice was shocking for being so matter-of-fact. 'He's not in that box. He's in you.'

Grandpa eased her away from me and helped her to stand straight.

'Take me home,' she said. 'The boy's alive. That will have to do. I shan't watch a box into the ground.'

Grandpa took her arm in his and they both walked off down the path towards the road.

The rose should have been thrown into the grave. Now she would keep it in a specimen vase till it died, when she would press it between the pages of the family Bible. She presented it to me years later, as though it were from a time before I was born. The handful of earth I picked up to throw splattered on to the surface of the coffin and lay there like a scab.

'The ride in the car,' I answered Mum. 'Both ways. The car ride out and the one back home. That was the best bit.'

'It's like a charabanc,' Mum had said. She laughed as she spoke, a laugh that soaked up into the heavy sombre clothing of those piled into the rear of the car. She enjoyed using English words for the first time, and I supposed this was one of them. The heater blew hard and steam was already beginning to rise, along with several complaints murmured quite loudly. They were tired of encroaching on each other's laps.

Mum slapped her hands on her knees to indicate we were ready to go. 'Take us to our house first, please. I think we need to change.'

It wasn't till I saw the windscreen wipers were no longer needed that I noticed the rain had stopped. Patches of blue sky let the sun dip through the clouds and light certain features. Houses, trees, whole horizons were picked out and lit against the backdrop of a sky that was still dark. I climbed on to Mum's lap to wipe my hand against the mist on the window. She wound the window down and looked out with me.

'What a beautiful day,' she sighed.

Six

On a walk with Dad one earlier summer we had been caught in a heavy shower. He taught me respect for lightning, that we shouldn't shelter under a tree. Instead we strolled along a country lane and got soaked. The shower passed. He hoisted me on his shoulders and turned off our path, marching us up an extra hill. The sun was out when we reached the top and a wind was blowing. He set me climbing an outcrop of rock and in minutes I was dry.

Now Dad was buried. I stood by my bedroom window and looked out as the final clouds rolled back. The sky was left a vivid blue. While Mum looked for a change of clothes in her wardrobe I picked up my bag of conkers and walked down the stairs. I didn't want to change. I wanted to run.

I headed for the wood that grew just outside our town. My favourite tree within it had a thick branch that stretched out close to the ground. It was strong enough to take my weight and bounce without breaking. On other days I liked to stand on it, bending my legs to make it spring ever higher till I leapt clear and into the space beyond. Now I simply sat on it, my feet off the ground, and gathered breath.

The tree marked the entrance to a meadow. Rays of sunlight were slanted like glass bars between the trees to mark its outer edges. A narrow stream had channelled its way through the ring of soft grass at its centre. I transferred the conkers from their plastic bag back to my jacket pockets and knelt down to scoop the bag full of water. Four holes punched in the bottom of it let the water out in thin streams. By the time I had run it to my first chosen spot the bag was almost empty, but I decided it didn't matter. The ground was still sodden with the morning's rain. It didn't need preparing.

I spaced the conkers out, judging how much space a full-grown tree would wish for itself, then walked round again to kneel beside each one and press it with my finger into the earth.

Beyond the wood, fields led up to a round grassy hill. At its top it dropped into a smooth hollow, like a crater lined in soft green velvet. It wasn't a volcano though. From the road on the other side, a track led directly to the hill. Edged with hedges so tall they were beginning to fold over and meet to form an archway, the track had once been laid with broken stones, but with the years these had sunk into the mud. Two broad weals scored the length of the track, ruts marked by the cartwheels of load after load of gravel pulled down from the hill by teams of horses. Once the pit had been worked and the gravel was gone, the site was left to nature to heal as best she could.

Dad had introduced me to the site. We had sat down with our backs to the hollow and looked out across the land just months before.

'We'll play a game,' he said. 'We're in the middle of the country, surrounded by nature. Agreed?'

I nodded.

'So look out there. Take a good look, and show me where there's no sign of man.'

It was easy. I pointed straight out in front of me.

Dad laughed. 'But there's a road there.'

'There's no one on it.'

'But someone built it. Show me where there's no trace of man at all.'

I took longer to choose a spot before pointing again.

'OK,' Dad agreed. 'Let's look over there. What's that blue thing?'

'A plastic bag.'

'So some man's been and left it there?'

'The wind could have blown it.'

'But now it's stuck.'

'It's caught on the fence.'

'A barbed-wire fence. Which didn't grow there naturally. Try again.'

I tried, but there was always a hedge or a telegraph pole or a footpath to spoil things.

'It's difficult,' Dad said, when I was close to giving up. 'But think hard. You can do it.'

I sat and thought, then twisted round to lie flat on my stomach and press my nose into the ground.

'Well done.' Dad laughed. 'What's it look like?'

'It's dark.'

'Pardon?' he joked, because my voice was muffled. 'I can't hear you.'

I sat up again so we could laugh together.

'You've found one way,' he said. 'Now here's another.'

He took hold of my shoulders and pulled me down till I was lying on my back, then lay down beside me.

'What do you see?' he asked.

'The sky.'

'Anything else?'

'Nothing.' There were no clouds, and the sun was on the other side of the hill.

'Once upon a time you would have seen branches and leaves. All of this land was covered with trees, then we chopped them down and turned the country into a park. One of the pleasantest things in life is lying on the ground and looking up through branches at the sky.

'But you're right, Tom. You're looking into the sky and you see nothing. Some people won't agree. They'll tell you that's where heaven is. They stare up into that nothing till they're full of it. It makes their bodies so light they can float about in the air. When they become as empty as the sky people call them holy and so don't need the sky any more. They can stare at the holy men instead.'

'But the sky's not really empty,' I challenged him. 'What about the sun and the moon and the stars?'

'This is your planet, Tom. Don't let the stars dazzle you. They're only there to show you the way. They're like words in a book. Learn how to read them and you'll never be lost. The whole universe is busy all the time, every star in every galaxy shifting itself through every moment, just so that you, Tomas Christie, can always tell exactly where you are on earth. That shows how important you are. Don't bother to question why you're here, Tom. Just get on and make the most of it for as long as time allows.'

He patted the level ground that formed the lip of the hollow.

'For now, shift up here and stretch your arms above your head.'

I did as he showed me.

'Now roll!'

He flicked my body round to tip it over the edge and I tumbled sideways down the slope, flashes of the earth and sky, light and dark whirling round to merge into one picture. I rolled on to my side when I got to the bottom and looked up. Dad was hurtling towards me, the grin on his face growing broader each time it revolved into view. I was looking into his eyes at the point we should have hit, then for a moment could see nothing, not the earth or sky, just the body of my father poised above me. He passed over and landed on the other side.

'That was great, Dad.'

He lay, trying to laugh but racked by coughs instead and gasping for breath in between them. He turned his head and watched as I scrambled back up the side of the hollow to the top.

'Let's do it again.'

I stood again where we had sat that summer. Below me two grey rabbits sat on the level bottom of the hollow, each absolutely still as though surprised by the autumn sunshine. It was too wet to sit so I crouched low and kept still to watch them.

They hadn't seen me, and the high walls of their hollow shielded them from sound. One rabbit raised and twitched its ears, alert to the day as much as to danger, full of a spirit it couldn't contain. The movement was a prelude to a dance.

For a few tremendous leaps the animal danced a solo, its body twisting round in short flights to keep itself company, then the other rabbit snapped out of its freeze. The two of them were hurled into a whirl. Like the blades of a propeller each movement left its image in the air till I couldn't see the rabbits for the dance, a dance with a shape so real I could shut my eyes and still see it. It was a reflection of the hollow, a grey inner wall charged into being by the energy of the creatures.

I can see it still. The sight was so immense I grew to contain it. As the rabbits slowed and the dance collapsed I had already stored it away.

It left me too full to take in the sounds from below. When I turned I saw a line of boys, all dressed in grey suits identical to my own. Those running at the head were already beyond the hedges and had started on the final climb. It was my class from school. I ran down the hill to head them off, opening my mouth but not daring to shout, my arms out to the side as though I could push them back.

The boy at the front stopped to give me space to slow my run down to a halt. It was Mark. We had become friends in the last few weeks.

'What's up?' he asked.

'Rabbits,' I half said, half whispered. 'Two rabbits. In the hollow.'

He bent low. For a moment I thought this was a rabbit imitation. It was the sort of daft thing he would do. Instead he motioned with his hands for the others to follow in line and began pacing up the hill. All the chatter ceased. The other boys watched and copied. As Mark picked up two stones from the track, they did the same. Veering left off the path to mount the hill at an angle his arms waved circles to signal the others to find their own way to the top. The line stretched and divided till the hill was surrounded.

I watched as they rose above me, and saw them creep more slowly as they neared the top. A girl who had been following the pack came and stood by my side as the ring of boys above us all lifted their fists of rock.

I began to run.

'No!' I yelled as I neared the top.

It was the cry they had all been waiting for. Some let fly immediately, the rocks from their young arms fairly powerless over such a distance, while others leapt over the rim to charge down into the hollow, roaring and screaming as they dropped towards the centre.

The rabbits were dizzy with panic. One threaded its body through the old movements of its dance, leaping towards openings only to see them closed as the boys' feet stamped towards it. The other, perhaps blind with fear, shot straight up the nearest bank. A boy's war-cry was squeezed into a yelp of surprise, his legs tangled as he tried to adjust his shot to the approach of the rabbit, and the animal ran clear just before the boy's falling back could squash it.

I can see its silhouette against the sky as it reached the far rim of the hollow, an image that's frozen though the rabbit never paused. The moment was pierced in my mind by a shriek from the hollow.

Dance has a shape, and terror has a sound. It's needle-thin. I heard it as the first rock smashed into the trapped rabbit's leg. Like the sting of a bee the shriek marked the end of life. Another rock hammered down on the creature's skull.

The boys walked back up the side of the hollow in file, a quiet procession that followed the long lean body of the rabbit. Mark held it by its ears. It hung in front of him, it thighs open and legs hanging low. He pushed it out towards me.

'Give it to your Mum,' he said.

Its body swung towards me as I took hold of its ears. They were cold. Their muscles crinkled in my hands.

'Normally they're shot and the bones are splintered,' Mark explained. 'You have to spit the gun pellets on to the plate like cherry stones. This should be good in a stew. We just hit the head and a leg.'

He wiped the palms of his hands against his trousers and looked around.

'What is this place in any case? We're meant to be finding out. Is it a volcano?'

'It's an old gravel pit. Too hard for rabbits to burrow into. That's why they couldn't escape. They'd just gone down there to play. The track you came up was for horses and carts to take the gravel away.'

It was all history now; the gravel pit, the rabbit, the dance. My class thought they had come up here on a history lesson, but you can never learn all about history. You create it as you go along. I felt dizzy as I stood and watched them run back down the hill.

The girl came up to stand beside me. She reached out a finger to touch the animal's fur, then snatched her hand away. The rabbit's head was flattened, like cartoon characters run over by steamrollers, only this job wasn't so clean. Its insides had burst out wherever they could. The sockets were thick with blood and gunge where the eyes had been.

The girl looked away to the woodland as tears wet her cheeks. She had ginger hair curled in ringlets at its ends, pink spectacle frames, a pale green dress, an open sky-blue hooded anorak, white kneecaps above long white socks, and sturdy black shoes and ankles that were caked in mud. Though the victim of someone else's tastes, in the mud and the tears and the fact that her anorak was undone there was hope.

'You're Dorothy,' I said.

She already knew that, so didn't bother to respond.

'We'll bury it,' she declared, with the authority that showed she was a headmaster's daughter. She raised the finger that had touched the rabbit and pointed to the wood. 'Over there.'

I started to walk down the hill towards the track, my arm crooked to hold the rabbit in front of my chest, and called to her without looking back.

'Go and kill your own.'

We walked back along the road to town, Dorothy walking beside me but trailing behind for safety whenever a car came along. One of the cars slowed down. Dorothy recognised it first and stopped. The driver's door on the far side opened and Mr Filey got out.

I was so close to the passenger door it couldn't open. Mum wound the window down and looked out.

The rabbit's feet rested on the outside of the car door as I pushed its head through the window.

'It's for you,' I said. 'We can eat it. Mark gave it to me. He's my best friend.'

Mum pulled the rabbit into the car and dropped it on the floor by her feet.

'That's kind,' she said.

Mr Filey stood on the road while Dorothy kept a few feet away from him, offering short answers to his barrage of questions. The girl had been left behind. Somebody was at fault. He was offering her the first chance to explain herself.

Mum leaned back to open the rear door and I climbed in.

'You've had us all worried,' she said, though calmly, turning to look over the top of her seat. 'Why didn't you say where you were going? I thought you'd gone to your gran's without me so I went there and now they all think you've run away. I ran to the school. Your class had gone off on a field trip and no one in the school had seen you. Luckily the bus came while I was still there and the boys said where they had left you. Mr Filey offered me a lift.'

'Why is Dorothy here?' I asked as the girl walked around the car to get in the other side.

'The boiler's broken down at her school and her mum's busy, so she joined your class for the day. It seems they forgot her.'

Mr Filey settled himself back into the driver's seat and turned to stare at me.

'Do you remember what I said to you in my office?' he asked. 'About responsibility for others?'

'Tomas isn't at school today,' Mum interrupted. 'His whole class, and their teacher, abandoned Dorothy in a field. Tomas refused to learn from their example, and was walking your daughter home. I think we should be grateful they have been found and that both are well, don't you?'

The smile she gave Mr Filey was so rich and true it silenced him. He turned the key in the ignition and drove us home.

Seven

Mum couldn't leave me alone on the way to school. She kept walking in front of me to adjust the peak of my cap or throttle me with the knot of my tie to set it straight. Given the choice she would have carried me all the way to keep the dust from my black shoes and leave them shiny.

'Now, remember,' she advised when we reached the school gates. 'Be polite. Be back by eight. Have a good time.'

She took off my school cap and adjusted the line of the parting in my hair before slipping the comb into my coat pocket. I ran across the schoolyard, glad that all her fussing had made me late. It gave me the excuse to hurry without looking back. There was just time to hang up my coat and line up for inspection.

'Nails and shoes!' Mr Filey commanded, and began his slow march down the line of boys as we held out our hands in front of us.

I was standing next to Mark. His nails were chewed-down stubs, his socks slack and his shoes scuffed, while the thinner strip of his tie hung below the band of his shorts. Mr Filey surveyed him from the shoes up to the tufts of his hair, the ones which seemed to grow backwards.

He clicked his tongue against the roof of his mouth and lengthened his face in sorry dismay.

'I will need to see your parents, Gifford.'

'What for, sir?'

'To see if your condition is genetic, or if there might be hope. For your sake, Gifford, I shall trust to find your parents both ugly and simple-minded. Then you might have a reasonable excuse for appearing the way you do.'

Mr Filey stepped aside from Mark to stand in front of me. He again started at the feet, but stopped when he reached my hands.

'There's no use holding your hands like that, boy. I know where they've been.'

I hadn't a clue what he meant.

'Your pocket flaps. Where are they?'

I pulled them out from the insides of my pockets and into view.

'What's the use of having pocket flaps if they're tucked out of sight? The evidence is against you, Christie. You've been idling. Idling with your hands in your pockets. You're a disgrace.'

He glared at me a moment then stepped back to address us

'You're all a disgrace. Every one of you. I've a good mind to leave you behind. Let's hear what you sound like before I make up my mind. Let me hear those voices. Do you see those clouds up there? When I call for cheers, I want a roar that punches a hole right through the middle of them. Are you ready? Hip hip!'

'Hooray!'

He looked up at the clouds, then held out his hand to feel for a spot of rain.

'You failed, boys. Try again!'

We practised till we had screamed ourselves almost hoarse, then fetched our coats and were led on our way with a stern warning not to kick through the last of the fallen leaves.

The motorcade was fifteen minutes late, and we were ten minutes early. We stood at the side of the road, stamped our feet, and tried to blow the air out of our bodies in smoke rings. When the black limousines came they came silently, almost slipping by before they could disappoint us. The true glory had already come before them, a posse of motorbikes with headlights like their own suns and a roar that stilled the limousines' purr to nothing. They were driving at the edge of the speed limit, in a bid to bring the royal party back on schedule. Pennants fluttered on the bonnets of each car, and inside them were the balding heads of men and the pastel-shaded hats of the women.

A final pair of motorbikes brought up the rear and the procession was gone.

'Which one was she?' a boy beside me asked.

He wanted to believe. He wanted to be told a story. I obliged.

'She was in the first car. In the pale pink. Didn't you see her smile and wave?'

'Of course I did. It had to be her, didn't it?'

Four sets of windows had driven by, and no one had looked out from any of them. They were talking amongst themselves. No one had waved.

'Wasn't she old!' I continued. 'And I didn't expect a princess to be wearing glasses!'

'How did you see all that?' the boy asked. 'They were going so fast.'

'That wasn't her fault. She leaned forward and tapped the driver on the shoulder to make him slow down but he couldn't. He had to keep up with the bikes. Weren't they great?'

The bikes were great. It was a fact. If you're going to lie, leave people room to agree. In any case my story wasn't really a lie. It was make-believe, which is where princesses belong.

The headmaster walked up behind us. He reached up and plucked a school cap from the otherwise bare branches of a tree, set it on Mark's head, and jammed it in place. Not a word was spoken. The clouds above us were still thick and threatened rain. He returned to the rear of our long crocodile to guard it on the silent trudge back to school.

The cheers that came from the other classrooms were strictly measured, disciplined roars in the silence. We looked up from our work each time, only to be stared back down by our class teacher. Our turn would come.

As Mr Filey entered the room we stood to attention. He sought permission from the teacher to interrupt the lesson, then stood to face us.

'I am gravely disappointed,' he declared. 'Who can tell me why?'

There was no response. I waited to be sure no one else would speak before raising my hand.

'Very good. Christie has something to say and we shall let him say it. Sit down, the rest of you.'

I lowered my hand and waited for them to settle.

'So, Christie. Give us your reason.'

'It all happened so quick, sir. The princess just flashed past.'

'Your mother is German, Christie. English, therefore, is not your mother tongue. That is your tragedy. Don't inflict it on us. Who can help the boy out?'

There were a few lame answers before he got the one he was looking for.

'Exactly. English is a fine language. Not every nation has need of its distinction and subtleties, but in English we observe a difference between adverbs and adjectives. "Quickly", Christie. "It happened so quickly." And princesses, in my opinion, seldom flash.'

There were titters from the class.

'You have increased my sense of disappointment, Christie, not explained it.' His tone silenced the class. 'Tell me, where was the princess being carried to at such speed?'

'To open an old folks' day centre.'

'Correct. And the party was late. Unlike you, who seem disappointed, I am delighted they swept on by. You're little more than infants, all of you. Wet behind the ears and as often as not wet between the legs as well. We have a task here in this school and it is massive. We are a junior school, charged with producing the most junior of citizens. Elsewhere in this town an institution has opened its doors to give respect and care to an entirely different order of humanity. Senior citizens. The princess knows her duty. She hurried on by because compared to those splendid folk who were already waiting for her this crowd of little boys did not merit the briefest attention. Sit down, Christie, stand up, Gifford.'

I sat down and Mark stood up.

'Gifford threw his schoolcap into a tree. Do you think that was clever?'

We didn't know what to think.

'I said do you think that was clever?'

'No, sir,' we chanted.

'No. It would have been clever had Gifford done so deliberately. That's the sort of cleverness that demands a rebuke, a prompt visit to the bonery. But Gifford didn't merely throw his cap into a tree. He threw himself into the moment. The one is a calculated move, the other instinct. What is instinct?'

A boy at the back put up his hand. 'When you can't help yourself doing something?'

'Like wetting your pants?' The boy had wet his pants the previous week. He was not well liked. 'Has anyone a better definition?'

The precedents for answering were not good. We all kept silent.

'Instinct draws a baby to its mother's breast, a lion to track its prey,' Mr Filey continued. 'It is the quality that keeps creatures alive in the natural world. Put up your hands who knows what the natural world is.'

A few boys raised their hands till we had all copied, stretching our fingers to point higher than each other. Mr Filey let us strain a while.

'Now put those hands down!' he finally snapped. 'I've no time to listen to your nonsense. None of you knows the natural world, do you hear me? None of you—unless your little minds stretch right back to the womb. What do you think you're doing here? Do these rows of desks and these walls seem natural to you?'

He let the questions float until we had all begun to look around the room.

'Of course they're not natural. Nothing to do with man is natural. He lives in a world of his own creation, only man is not God and so that world is a mess. In this school we have sealed off a little piece of that world to make it more manageable, with rules that can be written down and bells and uniform and inspections. It's a simple pattern of life for simple minds. We expand those minds, pray our prayers, sing our hymns, praise our Queen, so that when we step into the outside world we know how to behave. Today we stepped briefly into that world, and we failed. A princess passed before our eyes and we failed to respect her. Yours was a mindless act and we had rehearsed it. You were asked to cheer a rousing cheer, and you managed a baby's squawk. The princess ignored you. I despair of you.'

He walked to the door as though abandoning us, but then turned and faced us again from there. Mark was still standing.

'We decided you were a creature of instinct, Gifford. Is that something to be proud of?'

'No, sir.'

'Why not?'

'Because pride comes before a fall.'

'That's very pat, Gifford, but I would prefer you to think. It is all right to be proud if you know what to be proud of. We use instincts to survive. We lie and cheat and steal to survive. That is nothing to be proud of. Life can be divided in two, what is base and what is fine. The job of this school is to teach you the difference. Base instincts lead you to act for your own good, never mind anyone else. How do fine instincts differ? Anybody?'

He crossed his arms as a barrier against the returning silence.

'You need time to think? Very well, you shall have it. Take the weekend. By Monday I want five hundred words from each of you on "My finer instincts".'

'Does that include me, sir?' Mark asked.

'Explain yourself, Gifford.'

'I cheered, sir. I threw up my cap. You said that was good.'

'You're right, Gifford. You deserve special treatment. In the outside world you cheered a princess and you did well, for her light is so strong and we are so dim that rejoicing is better than envy. But that does not make you a princess. You want to separate yourself from everyone, to escape their punishment, when you've not yet learned to share their fate. The others can do me five hundred words. From you, Gifford, I expect a thousand. And make them fine ones.'

The teacher waited till the headmaster was out of the room before nodding permission for Mark to sit down.

Eight

Mr Filey reversed his old Humber across the playground to the main door of the school. The tyres splashed through puddles left by an earlier cloudburst to wheel a pattern across the asphalt.

I picked up one of two cardboard boxes that stood on the school step beside me, each holding a stack of light blue exercise books. Mr Filey took it from me and lodged it on the back seat.

'The first rule of combat. Know your enemy,' he quipped, and took the second box. 'Every weekend I take home samples of work to see how you're all doing. I suppose that surprises you?'

It didn't even interest me.

'People think we have an easy life, but no life need be easy. Teaching is a tremendous responsibility. Taken seriously, there's no harder or more rewarding job in the world.'

It was not a promising start to a conversation. I said nothing but waited for instructions. Mr Filey started the car and I followed it out of the schoolyard as told. I swung the broad iron gates closed, stamped the bolt into its hole in the concrete, and was driven back to Mr Filey's house for tea.

Mrs Filey was drying her hands on a tea-towel when she came into the hall.

'You are Tomas,' she announced happily, as though naming me for a part in a game. She hung the towel over her shoulder and came forward to take the satchel from my shoulder and hang it up. Then she held out her hand. I shook it.

'Oh, that's very proper!' Her voice was high and clear like a young girl's as she laughed. I held on to her hand and smiled. Her hair was piled high like a mushroom cloud, dark and bushy with a white streak above each ear. She was a wispy lady, her face pushed into high cheek bones above a narrow pointed chin as though it had spent a lifetime trying to laugh.

'You are a good boy,' she declared. 'I was only reaching for your coat.'

She helped it off my back and hung it up but kept on speaking.

'Now you know where we stay you can walk next time. I'm sure you don't want to linger on after school with Mr Filey, especially at the weekend. Come along through and meet Dorothy.'

Mr Filey was left to stand in the hallway, like a ghost who had got used to never being seen. He waited a few moments before drifting through to join us in the kitchen.

'I'll show Tomas the house,' he suggested. 'Take him up to my study.'

'Later, Lewis. Dinner's nearly ready. And Tomas is telling us all about the princess. It sounds like a really exciting day.'

'I wouldn't say that. She just flashed past, didn't she, Tomas? Not so much as a wave. For all I could tell she wasn't even there. It's not what one expects from royalty. The boys were very disappointed.'

'Tomas doesn't sound disappointed.' I had built up a thrilling tale of the princess waving at me alone. It was a story that begged to be believed. 'Maybe you're getting old. Maybe you've seen too much.'

'Maybe I expect too much,' Mr Filey conceded. 'But in my day...'

Lewis Filey was going to reminisce. Dorothy bent down to do the last sums of her homework on the kitchen table, and Mrs Filey turned to stir the saucepan on the stove.

We ate stew. Mr Filey supped the last spoonful of gravy, cleaned his spoon with a piece of bread, and set it back down to await his pudding. His wife picked it up to clear it away with his plate but he snatched it from her and slammed it back down on the table.

'One spoon's good enough for me,' he announced. He stared at me as he spoke. This was a gem of wisdom apparently spoken for my benefit. 'The girls are too pernickety.'

'It's just your excuse for not washing up,' Mrs Filey objected.

'Things don't need washing up. What's wrong with a bit of dirt? What are you afraid of?'

'Germs.'

'We're all family. Germs we can share. Germs won't hurt. Germans on the other hand! They were worth fighting against. All through the desert, Tomas, all through the war I carried my own cutlery, a knife, fork and spoon. Silver-plated they were. The other men laughed. Many of them supped straight out of a tin can. It became a joke, that cutlery, my own idiosyncrasy, but fine though they were I never washed them. I wiped them clean on whatever was to hand and they were ready to use again. I didn't wash them then, why should I wash them now? Just because I'm surrounded by fussy women? Never!'

'I'd like to know how many men died of disease,' Mrs Filey stated. 'More than a few, I'd be sure. How many got chronic dysentery? How many died of the runs? One week in Majorca last year, one evening meal in the hotel restaurant, and you kept to our room all the following day, scared to move far from the toilet in the bathroom. It's funny how we never hear of that side of your war.'

'It's not really a discussion for the dinner table.'

Mrs Filey took the chance to grab the spoon and fling it into the washing-up bowl. We heard it crack a glass.

'We have a dinner table,' she said. 'I'm glad you've noticed. I thought you were still picking food out of your desert fire. Now maybe you'll notice Tomas and me and Dorothy. We're not your men, Lewis. We don't need to live through your war anymore.'

Mr Filey stood up to fish the broken glass out of the water. He lifted the base of it out of the suds and then turned round to face us. Maybe he was going to use the glass to illustrate a point.

'Don't do that!' he yelled, and pointed at me with the broken glass.

He had warned me earlier against leaning back in my chair. I was doing it again, my kneecaps resting against the edge of the table. His shout made me jerk my kneecaps free. I reached forward to grab the table but my arms were left to spin circles in the air. Mr Filey shouted again but there was nothing I could do. I looked up at the ceiling and was floating.

'Oh God, Lewis.' Emma Filey didn't shout. It wasn't her way. The force in her voice was not volume but despair. 'Now look what you've done.'

All three of them looked. At first I could only see their legs but then Dorothy climbed down from her chair and the table was pulled aside. They looked nervous, unsure what would be revealed. I smiled to show no harm was done.

'Tomas,' Mrs Filey said, and then again. 'Tomas. Tomas. Tomas.' Each time the name was insistent, urging me to speak, but she left no room for me to do so.

'He's just a boy.' She stroked the hair back from my forehead, then left her hand to rest there as she turned on her husband. 'Why do you do it, Lewis? Why do you shout? Why do you have to be so fierce? We can't all take it. It breaks us apart.'

Mr Filey ignored her but gazed down at me. His body and head were still. Only his hands moved. He had picked up a tea-towel and was winding it round his wrist. He pulled it tight as I watched how the white of the cloth turned to red. The stain spread like a blot till there was too much for the cloth to hold. A drop fell on my cheek as Mr Filey leaned towards me.

The drop was soft, softer than water. It sat easily on my skin. I saw Emma Filey look at it, and noticed a fresh concern wash across her face.

I noticed everything, yet they say I was concussed. I spoke to ease their worries, yet they heard no more than sad sounds from my throat. My body had fallen from a chair and was left to play its part in a drama. There are times when life moves so swiftly it leaves us behind. The best we can do is witness.

'You're hurt,' Mrs Filey said, and her attention was drawn to her husband. 'Just look at you. You're bleeding all over him. What have you done?'

She reached for his hand, quickly at first to pull it away from my face then gently to care for the wound to his wrist.

'It's just a cut.' He placed his good hand on her shoulder to hold her back. 'I gripped the broken glass when I saw the boy fall. The stem sliced into my wrist. That's all. It's nothing.'

'What do you mean, it's nothing? Let me see.'

'See to the boy.' He stood up to be clear of her and fetched himself a clean towel out of the drawer.

'Look at his mouth,' Mrs Filey said. Her face loomed large as she stared at me. Her fingers touched my tongue. 'His teeth. His two front teeth. They've come out.'

She picked them out of my mouth and held them up as though for me to see.

'Dorothy, fetch a glass of water,' Mr Filey ordered. The girl hurried to do so as he knelt back down beside me. The new towel around his wrist wiped against the side of my face as he reached forward to lift my head. 'He turned as he fell. I heard his head crack against the floor.'

His fingers brushed my hair as he felt for the bruise. Dorothy brought the glass of water and he asked for the teeth to be dropped into it.

'You carry it, Dorothy. Carry the glass to the hospital. They might be able to plug them back in. You never know. There are so many miracles nowadays.'

'Oh dear,' Mrs Filey said. 'See how his nose is bleeding. Dorothy, run upstairs will you, love? Fetch us a cold flannel.'

She dipped her finger into the blood beneath my nose.

'Shouldn't we call an ambulance?'

'We'll drive him. It'll be quicker. The car's right outside.'

'You can't drive, Lewis. Not with that hand.'

'You can drive, can't you?'

'Not your car. You don't like me to drive your car. You say I make you nervous.'

'Do you think I care about the car? Do you think this is a time to be nervous? Stop worrying, woman. Go and get the keys.'

His arms reached beneath me. As he stood up he took me with him, cradled against his chest. His glasses had slipped down his nose. I could see above them to his eyes. They were small and grey, but as he blinked down at me they grew ever shinier.

We had been left alone for a moment. He spoke in a murmur, a voice that was just for us.

'Don't worry, Christie,' he said. 'I'll see you through.'

He arranged me on the back seat of the car. I lay across his lap with my head tilted back over his folded arm. His wounded hand pressed the cold flannel against my nose, and I gulped to swallow the blood that could not flow.

'We'll soon be there,' he assured me as the streets passed by outside. He turned his head to the window to check where we were, then peered up into the sky. 'What a night. It's so clear. The clouds have all gone. Do you know the stars, Christie? Let me show you. There's the Plough, look. That's the easiest to find. You can tell it's the Plough by...'

I tried to follow his words, looking through the open window at a sky spattered with infinite points of light that still left it dark.

'Don't let the boy freeze to death,' Mrs Filey called back. Dorothy was lost to sight on the front seat beside her. Her husband wound the window halfway up, then as I shivered closed it completely.

'You must go to the desert some day, Christie. Maybe I'll take you. That's the place to be if you want to see the stars. That's the place to be if you want to see life. There are none of these street lights to get in the way. No artificial lights at all. There's nothing artificial, Christie. Life's stripped back to its essentials so you know what life means. You wouldn't worry about this blood out there. It would seem right. You could be bathed in blood and simply be glad of having such a cool way to die.'

'Stop talking nonsense, Lewis. Nobody's dying.'

'A man died in my arms, Christie. I held him like I'm holding you now. His body shook, he went into tremors at the last, but he died in peace. There was more of his blood over me than was left in him. He was my best friend. He still is my best friend, even though he's dead. But I'm not sorry he died. His death was natural. I didn't want him to live. I wanted to die too, Christie. I wanted to die too.'

'Please be quiet, Lewis. Don't ramble on. Don't go back to your desert. Not now. The boy's hurt. Not now.'

'I saw a donkey, Christie. A dead donkey. It lay on its back at the side of the road. Its legs were stuck up in the air, stiff they were, as though the animal were stuffed. We passed it in our jeep every day for three days. On the fourth day the animal had company. Three other donkeys stood around it. They brayed, Christie. How they brayed. They held back their heads, and a sound came out like I've never heard since. It was a clear sound, a rasping sound, like the wail of a siren but touched with grief. You learn that too in the desert, Christie. You learn how death is part of life. It lives on. There are no ghosts, Christie. It's you and me who haunt the world. We carry old deaths within us.'

He shuddered.

'It's cold, Christie. It's growing very cold. I'll keep you warm. Let me hold you tight.'

I could feel him trying to hug me close, though the pressure in his arms was not really there.

'Don't worry, Tomas,' Mrs Filey said. 'This is the hospital now. We'll have you inside in a moment.'

She pulled the car up in front of the main doors. The neon light from the hospital foyer spilled into the car. Mr Filey opened his door then gathered me more firmly in his arms before sliding along the seat and standing up.

The doors to the hospital opened either way. They could be pulled or pushed. Mr Filey chose to push. His feet stopped and he leaned forward to squeeze me between his chest and the glass. Our combined weight eased the door back. I looked up into Mr Filey's face to try and understand what was happening. His eyes looked shocked then vacant, a glaze passing over them to cover all emotions from view, but he held on tight as we collapsed gently to the ground. Somehow he turned as we fell so that I had a soft landing on top of his body.

I was inside the hospital, though Mr Filey's legs stuck out through the door to keep it ajar. Through the gap I could see the car with its doors flung open. Emma Filey's face opened in horror. First she sucked the sight in, then let it out again in a scream that sent her running towards us. Dorothy followed behind, more curious and casual, and stood a few yards back to watch.

Mrs Filey picked me up and held me towards the light. I looked back at her white blouse, newly smeared with red patches, up at her startled eyes, then down at myself. What had started the day as a smart school uniform was now totally stained in blood.

'Is Daddy dead?' Dorothy asked.

It was a little girl's question. It didn't surprise me, but then I was a little boy. Life's nothing but surprises at that age. Death's no more puzzling than anything else.

'Daddy's dead,' Dorothy insisted, and tugged at her mother's skirt till she had to look down and take notice. I was dropped with such speed that my legs buckled and I lay on my back on the floor. More faces came and looked down on me, picked me up, laid me on a trolley and wheeled me away beneath a row of lights sunk into the ceiling.

The women's voices were soft beside my bed. They were talking about me. I kept my eyes closed so as not to interrupt them.

'It's good to see him sleeping,' Emma Filey said. 'I love to see children asleep. They look so innocent.'

'He is innocent,' Mum said. 'No one's saying he's not, are they?'

'Oh no, I didn't mean that. I didn't mean to suggest anything. Tomas is not to blame for what happened. Not at all. It was an accident. A heart-attack, the doctors say. Lewis was never strong. Such loss of blood, and the sudden worry, it was all too much for him.'

She was silent a moment, gathering the thoughts she wished to speak.

'When I saw him there, saw your son sitting on top of my husband, my legs almost gave way. I wanted to flop down to the ground. He was blinking at me. Your son was blinking at me, the whites of his eyes so clear in the bloody red mess of his face. He looked like a demon. A friendly little demon with a red skin, even his hair sticking out from his head like flames.'

Mrs Filey began to cry, her breath shuddering from her body to be gulped noisily back in. Mum murmured words of comfort, then they both drew breath and seemed to be looking at me again.

'I'm sorry.' Mrs Filey took in a slight hiccough of breath. 'He's not a demon, of course. He's an angel.'

'He'll look strange without his front teeth.'

'I'm so glad they were baby teeth. You were right. We do that. We worry about little things like baby teeth staying in too long. Do you think there's always a reason for these things, if we wait long enough to find out?'

The question was a good one, but an answer would have to wait. Emma Filey started to cry.

'Cry,' Mum encouraged her. 'You cry. Cry.'

'He was talking about the war,' Mrs Filey said, when she had snatched enough breath. 'His war in the desert. I tried to make him stop, but he wouldn't listen. He talks that way at night. He talks that way in his sleep. I'm used to it, I just lie there and wait till it's all over, but it's not good for a young boy to hear. I asked him to stop. He was talking about death all the time. He talked about dying. Do you think he knew?'

'Don't talk about it. Don't worry. It's over now. It's nobody's fault.'

The talk and the crying eased itself into silence. I opened my eyes to check that they were still there. Mum and Mrs Filey were wrapped in each other's arms. Dorothy stood a little behind them.

'Tomas,' Mum said when she saw me, and pulled herself away from Mrs Filey.

I smiled back at her. The smile hurt my face. Mum only hesitated a moment before reaching to brush the hair from my forehead but I noticed she was shocked. We see ourselves in others' faces. I decided not to smile for a while.

'How do you feel?' she asked. 'Would you like to go home?'

I nodded.

'They've lent you a dressing-gown.' It hung over the back of the bedside chair. 'We'll take you home in that. We can send it back with the pyjamas tomorrow.'

A nurse had bathed me. Her cupped hand had trickled water over my head. It ran down my body to turn the bath pink. When I was dried she had put me into a pair of striped pyjamas and walked me to a bed.

'I'll give you a lift,' Emma Filey offered.

'Thank you, but no. We'll take a taxi.' Mum's refusal was too abrupt, and she tried to soften it. 'We don't want to trouble you. You've had too hard a day. You must want to get Dorothy home to bed.'

'It won't take us five minutes.' Mrs Filey looked around and spotted the plastic carrier bag that held my dirty clothes. A moment later she was clutching it. 'I'll carry these. Come on, Dorothy. Take my hand. We're going to take Tommie and his mother home. We'll see where they live. Then tomorrow we can visit them.'

Mum pulled back my bedclothes and lifted me into her arms. She walked in silence along the ward. As we approached the swing doors the sound of Mrs Filey's heels clicked on past. She pushed the door open with one arm and pressed Dorothy against the wall to leave our path clear.

Nine

The love of two women can do more than wake a child, but it woke me that morning. It was my first glimpse of its power.

My favourite pyjamas, patterned with miniature soldiers in red tunics and black busbies, lay opposite me in the bed. Dorothy was wearing them. She opened her eyes to look into mine, then we both turned to look at the mothers standing inside the bedroom door.

The two women smiled and their eyes were bright with tears. They should have separated, each mother moving to a side of the bed to claim her own child into the morning. Instead they turned from us. They faced each other with their smiles before stepping back from the room.

We waited to see if they would return, then climbed from the bed. We were in Mum's bedroom. I led Dorothy down the stairs and into the kitchen.

'Here they are,' Emma Filey said. 'Our Babes in the Wood.'

I smiled, a smile broad enough to open my mouth wide. They looked shocked, but it was the shock of schoolgirls being caught with a midnight feast, one swiftly followed by laughter.

'Oh, I'm sorry, Tomas,' Mum said, and wiped her eyes with the back of her hand. 'We mustn't laugh.'

'At least they were baby teeth,' Emma Filey said. 'New ones will soon grow in. They were front teeth too. We mustn't forget that. They're worth a lot of money. Your Mummy tells me you don't sell teeth to the fairies. I was pleased to hear it. I'd like them for myself. Is half a crown all right?'

She had fetched the coin out of her purse. I nodded and reached out for it.

'That's good.' She stood up as the deal was concluded and reached for a figure from the work surface. It was modelled from green plasticine, but had its back to us so I could only see the bobble of its tail. 'I've made this for you.'

She brought it down to stand on the kitchen table. It stood on two large splayed feet. Its body and head were like a green snowman's, one smaller ball plonked on top of a large one. Arms with no hands stuck out from its body, and plasticine of the same size stuck up from the head as ears. Dots served for the eyes and thin strands were stuck on as whiskers.

'Now I can finish it.' Mrs Filey pulled a small parcel of tissue paper from her purse. Inside it were my two front teeth. She picked them out and jammed them into the creature's face.

'There,' she said, and turned it round as though proud of what she had done. 'A bunny rabbit.'

The teeth were stuck on at an odd angle to each other, as though the creature had grinned once and distorted its face for life.

'Isn't he cute?' Mum said, and joined Mrs Filey in smiling down at the monster.

I checked with Dorothy. She looked at the rabbit, and then up at the two women, awaiting an explanation.

'That's very kind of Mrs Filey,' Mum said. 'What do you say?'

'Thank you.'

'There's a good boy. Now you come up here. I need my morning hug.'

As I climbed on to Mum's lap Emma Filey held out her arms for Dorothy.

'What are they doing here?' I asked.

'Mrs Filey slept in your bed last night,' Mum explained. 'And I slept on the couch.'

There was no telling why. Like spending the night in a tent in your own back garden, the logic was not important. There was simply the adventure of the thing.

'We're going to get dressed, then Mrs Filey's driving us back to her house for breakfast.'

'Not Mrs Filey. Emma,' Mrs Filey suggested, then wondered how it might sound from the mouth of a child. 'You can call me Aunt Emma.'

We were allowed into Emma Filey's garden to play while the two women spoke over coffee in the front room. It was a while before they came to find us.

Emma was carrying a jug of water and a sponge. She stood still with her head held high. It was the way someone would stand and sense rain before it fell. With her sponge she was ready to mop it up.

'What have you done?' she asked.

She looked at the knife and spoon in my hand, taken from her kitchen drawer and now smeared with soil. The clue gave away more than I expected. She walked straight to the middle of her neat square lawn and knelt down.

'We buried it,' Dorothy said. I had sworn her to silence but she was too excited to keep the secret. 'We buried the green rabbit. I fetched one of Daddy's hankies and we used it as a shroud. I told Tomas we shouldn't dig in the lawn but he says graves are covered with grass. His daddy's grave's been covered with grass. Will that happen to my daddy too?'

'Daddy's being cremated,' Emma Filey said. 'He wants us to burn him.'

She wasn't thinking of the words as she spoke them. She was studying the damage to her lawn.

'We were very careful,' I told her. 'I cut the grass with the knife and rolled back the turf. You can hardly tell that we dug there, can you?'

She looked at me, then stood up.

'Oh, well. Never mind,' she sighed.

She walked over to the birdbath with a stone bird perched on its rim and dropped in the sponge to soak up the previous day's water. Then she carried it over to a bed of pruned roses to squeeze it dry.

'Lewis wasn't a gardener. He liked the desert. Given the choice, I sometimes think he'd have turned the garden into a sandpit. But he did come out here and sit sometimes. It's a lovely place to collect yourself. Try it, Margaret. Sit down.'

She indicated a wooden garden bench. Mum moved towards it while Emma soaked the last of the birdwater into her sponge. She squeezed it out over the flowerbed once again.

'These gave a lovely display this year. Do you like roses, Margaret?'

Mum nodded and smiled.

'I'll rake Lewis's ashes into them. He used to say he wanted them scattered over the Libyan desert, but that was just a joke, wasn't it? He wouldn't expect me to fly out there? I'm sure it's better if the ashes do some good.'

There was a silence till Mum chose to break it.

'I am sorry about your lawn,' she repeated.

'Oh, that doesn't matter.' Emma poured the fresh water from her jug into the birdbath. 'I'm silly about this garden really. I don't let anyone else touch it. It's like my sanctuary. But Tomas wasn't to know that. You must come early one morning and help me feed the birds, Tommie. It's not much of a garden in this season, but you'll see what I mean when the birds flock down. They really bring the garden to life.'

'I'm surprised you want him back,' Mum said. 'What a strange thing to do. Why did you have to bury that nice rabbit?'

'It was dead.'

'How did it die?'

'You saw it. It was hideous. It had to die.'

'Oh, that's horrible, Tomas. That's an awful thing to say. I don't think I like you this morning.'

She closed her eyes and crushed her hands between her knees as she took a deep breath. Then she questioned me again.

'Why did you bury it? Rabbits don't get buried.'

'Not normally. Normally they die in their burrows so they're buried already. That one needed help.'

'Rabbits die where they die.' Mum looked up at the sky and spoke for a while into the clouds until her story got going. 'I was cycling just out of town years ago when I had to get off my bike. The road was too full of dead rabbits for me to continue. Some still lived. Blind they were, all blind. The sight was leaking out of their eye-sockets. Spasms in the hind legs of one of them shot it forward into my front wheel. I screamed and dropped the bike to run away. This is where the bike caught me.'

She reached down to point to the scar on her calf. Emma was about to sit down on the seat beside her, but paused to bend and run her hand along the scar's puckered skin. Mum pulled her leg back then gave a quick smile to show she wasn't really upset. Emma settled herself on to the seat and Mum continued.

'It was a shock. Of course they were only rabbits, but it isn't only rabbits we treat that way. We do the same to people. It brought back too many memories. When I got far enough away I fell down on the grass verge and vomited, then I felt much better. I picked my way back through their bodies to collect my bike and pedalled on. When I got home my shoe was full of blood.'

She saw that Dorothy and I hadn't understood.

'It was myxomatosis,' she explained. 'A disease man gave to rabbits when he decided there were too many of them. Millions of them died a horrible death. I only got this scar.'

She looked up from examining her scar afresh and laughed to break the tension when she saw how serious we both looked.

'Why do rabbits have big ears?' she asked.

I sensed a joke, like *'Why do humming-birds hum? Because they don't know the words'*. I shook my head.

'So they can hear any danger from far away.'

To want to tell a joke you have to know one. Mum had better uses for her time.

'I think you will love this garden,' Emma Filey said. She was following her own train of thoughts. 'You can treat it as your own. You too, Tommie. Come here.'

She opened her arms for me to climb onto her lap. Mum received Dorothy in the same way.

'This is a horrid time,' Aunt Emma said. 'But we'll see each other through. I think we're all going to be great friends. Don't you?'

Mum's and Aunt Emma's smiles were genuine if sad. Dorothy's was broad because she was trying so hard to join in. I kept my mouth shut so they could forget about my missing teeth.

Ten

Gran had waited a long time to visit Coventry. The January day she finally chose showed the city in its true colours. They were the various hues of dusty grey.

We left the bus station to walk around the town. Christmas was dead but its remains still littered the shops. Escalators carried Gran and me between the floors of Owen Owen the department store, where tired shoppers wandered between stalls scattered with the last tat of the sales, and strip lighting revealed the bareness of the concrete structure. The illuminations were still strung across the street outside, a tangle of wiring that no longer bothered to light up the embossed plastic images of Father Christmas and his reindeer.

Snow had begun to fall, dropping as flakes but turning to sludge as it hit the streets. Gran made a vice of her hand and gripped my fingers till the bones cracked, anxious that I should not slip and fall. We both hesitated as we walked the streets, shuffling tiny steps to keep our balance and stay abreast of each other. We were heading for the cathedral.

Cathedrals are about space as much as anything, vast chambers of emptiness set down in the heart of a city where they wait to become hallowed. Masons and stonecarvers can give the first spiritual charge but after that the constant murmur of prayer must soak into the cathedral walls.

The people of Coventry have got a lot of praying to do.

Perhaps the air was still burnt dry before they tried to contain it. Gran led me into a space that was vast, but surrounded only by walls of flimsy honey-coloured bricks. Individual pine chairs were lined up in rows instead of the solid pews I had expected from our own town church. Gran led me round them to view a large tapestry. It had been in the news, it was controversial; I have learned since that it was by Graham Sutherland, but I have not been back to see it. I have only my memory as a boy to go by. It took of the colours of Coventry.

The tapestry was large and grey, like a poster tacked on to the giant walls. The body was of Christ before the resurrection. Maybe the city was still too close to the firestorm. It didn't want to have its faith rekindled just yet.

'We stood in our garden and watched it burn,' Gran repeated once we were back on the pavement and outside the charred remains of the old cathedral.

The altar, with its cross forged from nails salvaged from the ruins, was visible from the street. The building was still brooding. I imagined a bonfire so big Gran had had to wait till now to come and kick over its embers.

'It was like Guy Fawkes' Night had come a week late. Your dad swore he could feel the heat, though that was just him being silly. He wanted to be part of everything, did Douglas.

I went inside to get out of the cold and stare through the kitchen window, but he stayed out on the lawn shivering at the sight.

'There's a mass grave around here somewhere. They couldn't tell one body from the other, they were that badly burned. I suppose there was no one left to do the recognising either. They just built one big hole and dropped them all in.

'We'll have to look for that another time, though. If we don't hurry we'll miss the show.'

We had bought the tickets that morning. Among the last left, the seats were perched high in the gods. I had never heard of 'the gods' before. It seemed marvellous to get to climb so high. Gran took the stairs gradually. Though she never spoke out I saw the tears of pain in her eyes as we reached the top. Those tears are still my best understanding of what arthritis is. She smiled at my laughter as the show started. The pantomime was *Jack and the Beanstalk*. It starred Ken Dodd and a happy band of tiny Diddy Men that danced about him waving the bright feathers of their tickling sticks in gay salute as the beanstalk spiralled up into the sky. Then we set off back through the snow to our bus and the journey home.

'That's the very best day I've had this year,' I quipped, with the year just two days old.

'That's good,' Gran said.

The heater on the bus was thawing her bones and she smiled with pleasure. She hadn't got the joke but had taken a compliment instead, so I chose to be satisfied.

It's thanks to Gran that I knew who Ken Dodd was. Mum wouldn't let a television into the house.

'What's wrong with books?' she said when asked to defend the stance, but she had a private reason for rejecting TV.

She hated war films.

We spent Sunday afternoons at Gran and Grandpa's. They had a television set. I liked to linger in front of it till it was time to go home to bed, and Gran would happily have let me sit there till I dropped off to sleep and she could have carried me upstairs, never to let me go.

They wanted us to sell up our home and move in with them. They wanted to make one happy family out of the four of us. They didn't like to think of Mum bringing me up on her own.

'Then try not to think of us at all,' Mum wanted to say. 'We shall survive quite happily without you.'

Sunday lunch was the compromise.

On our first visit we ate roast beef, then settled in front of the television. A war film started. Mum sat silently through the first half of it, but we could all sense the tension mounting inside her. Finally she let it go.

'This is such a lie,' she said.

'How would you know?' Gran asked sweetly. 'You couldn't have been told the truth. Not in Germany. Not during the war.'

'What truth?'

The scene on the television showed an RAF pilot on a visit from base to take afternoon tea in the parlour of his mother's cottage.

'You couldn't have asked that question,' Gran said. 'Not if you had lived here. There's only one truth. If you had known it there wouldn't have been a war. That's what war is all about. Teaching stubborn people the truth.'

'If you like truth so much, how can you sit in front of this?' The mother on the TV screen poured tea into two china cups and Mum pointed at her, her whole arm outstretched. 'Country cottages. Chintzy tea parties. Noble heroes. It's a lie.'

'It's England,' Gran countered.

'It's obscene.'

'He'll die,' Grandpa said, as though the tension had built up out of concern for the plot. 'He'll fly off on a mission and be killed. That's why we're seeing how lovely things are at home. It's showing us how horrible war is.'

'War is as horrible as a spoiled tea party?' Mum countered, a question like a dambuster's bomb designed to bounce and bounce till it hit the target. She kept silent till the pilot had returned to base and the call to scramble came through.

'Come on, Tomas.' She stood up. 'We're going home.'

'What? Before the film's finished?' Grandpa still had some idea that he was innocently digesting a big lunch in front of a simple film. He had not noticed that the battleground had shifted to our front room.

'Why, what happens next?' Mum asked him. 'Will he be shot down now?'

'Not straight away. He's got his mission to accomplish first.'

'So he'll drop his bombs on target?'

'He's a good pilot.'

'And die a hero?'

'I should hope so.'

'He'll vanish from his plane and be spirited up to heaven while good citizens are blown apart below him and the land bursts into flames. Now we know what happens, there's no need to stay.'

'But Vera's got your tea in.' Grandpa nodded towards his wife. 'She's made a salad. The tomatoes and radishes are already cut. She's crinkled the edges. And there's a tin of crab I'm going to open.'

'We've already had a lovely meal, thank you.'

I was sharing a seat with Gran. She put her hand on my shoulder.

'Leave Tom,' she said.

'Tomas, put your coat on. We're going home.'

'No, leave Tom.'

'Leave my son to watch this? What kind of a mother do you take me for?'

'There's no harm in it.'

'There is harm in it. You don't know. It's so English that you can't see. You believe that if something is nice it must be right, if something is sentimental it must be true. Don't you think we have these films in Germany too? Every country has these films. Only in Germany, and I pray this is true, we know where these films can lead us. We know how offensive they are.'

'Then go back to Germany.'

'And take Tomas with me?'

'Leave Tom. Leave Tom where he belongs.'

'Tomas belongs with me.'

'Now that is a lie.' Gran kept silent for a moment, sensing triumph but not knowing where it would take her. 'Do you think Douglas belonged to me?'

'Always.'

'Never. Children never belong to their parents. Do you think I would have let him go to war? Would I have let him go to Germany? Do you think I couldn't guess what life was like there? I couldn't imagine it, I'll give you that. It outstripped my imagination. That was the worst of it. I imagined things to be as bad as I could, but knew they were worse even than that. And I had to send my son to that place. He was much too sensitive to survive. Simply reading about the war in the papers and listening to it on the radio scarred him horribly. Sending him to Germany was like trying to seal a wound with a naked flame. Your country drained him. It sucked out his spirit and then sent him home.'

'How can you say all that, then watch rubbish like this?'

Mum waved her hand at the TV set. The orchestra was stirring up waves of rising chords as the first planes swooped towards their target.

'It's so neat. A beginning, a middle, and a comfortable end. That's not what war's like. That's not what life's like.'

'Then let us watch the film in peace. If it's not like war, it can't trouble us. Tom's young. He's new. He's a little child.

It's a blessing he can enjoy a film like this. He doesn't want to be churned up like you. You've had a rough life, Margaret, but it's your life. Don't wish it on your son.'

Exhausted of words, they both stared at me a while.

'Do you want to stay for tea?' Gran asked.

I nodded. If Mum had asked if I wanted to go straight home with her I would have nodded too. Instead she told me to take care since I would be walking home in the dark, and Grandpa pushed himself out of his chair to show her to the door.

Mum and Gran had more to say to each other, but they had tired themselves out. It was more than two years later, in the summer of 1966, that their conversation resumed. The occasion was a rare one, when Mum chose to sit alongside us in front of the television one Saturday afternoon. England were at home to West Germany in the World Cup Final.

The curtains were drawn against the glare of the sun. Grandpa had two bottles of beer beside his armchair but no glass. He would drink from the bottle, he told me. That was the way to enjoy a football match. Two bottles of Coca-Cola were set on the floor beside my seat so I could copy him, while Gran used half-time to go and make herself and Mum a fresh pot of tea. She managed to do the same again in the few minutes before extra time, then both women had to rush to the toilet as the teams changed ends for the final fifteen minutes.

I best remember two scenes from the game. First the shot from Geoff Hurst that struck the underside of the crossbar, hit the ground, then leapt back towards the centre spot. I thought balls had to land in the back of the net. This wasn't how I understood goals to be.

It put England into the lead. Outside the house the summer was at its most glorious, though its light was shut out by the curtains. As West Germany equalised in the closing moments a further half-hour stretched ahead.

Then I remember Nobby Stiles skipping along the edge of the pitch with the lid to the cup balanced on his head. He was not much taller than a kid and his grin displayed a set of teeth more wayward than mine. He was the picture of a man reduced to happiness. That wasn't how I understood men to be.

He was certainly happier than Mum.

'If only Churchill were around to see this!' Gran crowed as Bobby Moore raised the World Cup over his head.

I knew about Churchill. I had learned about him in two recent lessons from Gran's TV. In one I had watched an old man wheeled to a window where he smiled and raised a hand to thousands of people packed in the street below. They had come to celebrate his ninetieth birthday.

'Who is Churchill?' I asked.

'He was Prime Minister during the war.'

'Why are there so many people?'

'They've come to say thank you. He saved us. He is the most important man in the country. Probably in the world.'

'What about the Queen?'

'She was just a girl. He saved her too.'

Not long afterwards I sat and watched the man's funeral procession unwind through the streets of London. The people who had packed the street outside his house now lined the road. They were less excited because they had got what they were looking for. The man had been too old at his birthday party, but now he had come out on the streets to play.

'You don't look too pleased, Margaret. We've won. England has won.'

Gran was trying to coax a reaction from Mum, but I doubted if it would be joy.

'Perhaps she's *not* too pleased?' Grandpa suggested. He had a kind way of being rational, spelling out the obvious as though there were no emotion involved. 'You've got to have mixed feelings when your mother country plays your adopted one.'

'It's not her mother country. It's the fatherland. You wanted them to win, didn't you? You wanted Germany to win.'

'It's only a game. It doesn't matter to me.'

Mum had clenched her hands in her lap and sat rigid through most of the match, trying to hold her reactions inside herself.

'Germans don't play games.' Gran was playing a game of her own, the game of breaking Mum down. 'They play to win.'

'And we've lost again,' Mum chanted in a silly sing-song voice. 'We lost the football game and we lost the war.'

'You said it,' Gran declared, and looked smug.

'Now now, ladies,' Grandpa put in, like a referee recalling two boxers to their corners. It was obvious the fight was going to continue, and the next round would be the last, fought to the death, all rules forgotten, the referee thrown clear of the ring.

'You go outside, Tomas,' Mum said. 'It's a lovely day and a pity to waste it. Run outside and play.'

I had walked to Gran's in my football boots, but taken them off in the hall. I was to meet friends for a real game of our own once the match was finished. I got up at once, said goodbye as I left, and sat down in the hall to put my boots on.

They did not talk for a while, leaving the chatter to the commentators on TV. My lace snapped as I pulled to do it up. I pulled it all out to try to knot and rethread it. They must have presumed I was gone.

'Tom was pleased,' Gran said. 'He got excited in the right places. He cheered when he was meant to. He's a proper little English boy.'

'Good,' Mum answered. 'That's good.'

'You've never really settled here, have you?'

'My married life was here. I have a home, my child, my friends. What do you mean?'

'You're not settled. You're not an easy woman to be with. There's a huge part of you always wanting to be somewhere else. We don't satisfy you here in England. You still live for your past.'

'I have no past.'

'You're nothing but your past. I could sense it there beside me all through the game. There wasn't an atom of you that wanted England to win. For all you deny it, you're as German as they come.'

Gran could have been stating a simple observation, but she spat it out as an insult.

'I don't deny it.' Mum's voice was strangely calm. 'I have never denied that I am German.'

'You don't admit it either. You keep it bottled up inside. Why didn't you cheer when Germany scored? That would have been honest.'

'I didn't want to cheer. I was pleased. I felt pleased. It's the first time I've felt pleased to be German, probably in all my life, and do you know what? It frightened me. It brought back too many memories. It's good that England won. They needed to. I like to see so many happy people.'

'You could look more pleased.'

'Very well. I shall smile.'

Mum presumably bared a grin, for I heard Gran tut with displeasure.

'Tomas can visit you on his own in future,' Mum announced. 'It's obvious that you don't like me. But always remember, Tomas is my son. Since I am German, your grandson is half German too.'

'Now don't say that.' Grandpa stirred himself in his chair to join in. 'Don't give us that nonsense about staying away. You know you're always welcome. We love to see you, both of us. Vera's always moaning that you don't come round more often.'

'That's kind of you, Eric, but you know that's not true. Don't worry. I won't keep Tomas away from you. He loves you, you love him. That's good. You don't like me. That's fine. I can accept it. I shall stay away.'

'You're wrong there, girl.'

'You don't think I was a good wife for your son.'

'That's different,' Gran interrupted, ready to take a stranglehold on the conversation. 'That's different to not liking you. You can like roast beef and you can like custard, but it doesn't mean they go well together. The war hurt Douglas. It changed him. He was always vulnerable, always too sensitive for his own good. As he grew up we managed to toughen him up a bit. He could have got on in life if that war hadn't come. It knocked all the ambition out of him. When he came back with a wife in tow we thought well, at least he'll settle down to something now. And I suppose he did. He became a postman!

'I don't know what he saw over in Germany, he never did tell all of it, but it knocked all the guts out of him. That's all I know for sure. The light went out of his eyes. He didn't care anymore. I'm not blaming you, Margaret, really I'm not. You had too much misery of your own. Douglas needed someone to help him forget. Someone less fierce. Someone less intelligent. Some simple English girl he could make happy.'

'We made one wrong move,' Mum said. 'We came back. Douglas needed longer away from this country. I didn't understand how difficult it is for a man to break away from his mother.'

I sat on the floor of the hall, holding the lace to my boot and keeping still so they would not hear me. The television was still on. They seemed to be watching it for no one spoke for some minutes. Then Grandpa got out of his chair and turned it off.

'I think you're right, Margaret love,' he said. 'You'd best be going.'

They held another long silence before Mum spoke.

'Shall I tell you?' she asked.

The springs on Grandpa's chair creaked and the air wheezed out of its cushions as he sat himself down again.

'I'll tell you my story. Our story. You'll never know otherwise. You know how we met. How I was a secretary who had to type up the reports he wrote on his sector of Berlin. But the story goes back further than that.

'I grew up in Dresden. I've told you that much. You know about Dresden. It burned my childhood out of me. My parents died there. You say Douglas shouldn't have gone to Berlin. Well, neither should I. I should have died in Dresden along with everyone else.

'My mother's sister, Aunt Hedwig, must have been one of the first to go. Her home was ripe for burning. The front room was lined with books, row upon row of them packed from the floor to the ceiling into mahogany shelves. They were in English, most of them. Every week a fresh parcel arrived from her booksellers in London. She had little money, my aunt Hedwig, but many books. She felt sorry for the English, she said. They had some of the richest literature in the world, but not a clue how to appreciate it. She thought of those parcels of books as refugees. Anyone was welcome to sit in her room and study them. Bringing German readers to English writers was like bringing a match to the candle, she said. A candle only shows its true glory when it begins to melt.

'She must haunt that library still, wondering what went wrong. Or maybe the library haunts the city.'

Mum snorted, like half a laugh, but could not pause for long as there was only her to do the talking.

'She taught me to read. She stuffed me with as much love and knowledge of those books as I could hold. When the authorities needed someone who knew English to go to Berlin they came for her. She had a young family. They're all dead now, of course, so it needn't have mattered, but at the time she felt she couldn't leave them. She recommended me to go in her place, and I agreed.

'I travelled to Berlin, found my room, then went in search of the department where I was to report for work. It wasn't there. I found the street; the street name was fixed to a building on the corner; but a hundred yards further and the street disappeared. There was a crater where the road should have been, and to either side nothing but rubble.

'I know you suffered in the war. Your town was bombed but it wasn't blasted, not day after day, yesterday's ruins smashed ever closer to the ground. I only began to understand it as I stood in that road. The smell hit me first, the stench of phosphor and gas that packed my lungs. Then the waste, acres of rubble and blackened metal, the city collapsed and all sense gone, and I sank to my knees for the space was so dizzy. Someone had climbed a pile of rubble to my right to plant a swastika flag. It was a human touch in a way. It was comic, horribly comic. I sobbed and howled till I ached too much to move, lay on the road to rest, then walked home.

'That was my war. It began and ended at that moment. There was no point crying or feeling it any more. If I survived one raid, there were five more hours to live before the next. That was as much as anyone knew.

'Home was a room in my grandmother's house, my mother's mother. The house was large. It could hold two of our Dresden families for summer holidays if we all squeezed together. Now the men were at war and there was just my grandmother left. I had a room to myself, big enough for my bed and a table and chair, and the rest of the house was filled with women who had lost their homes.

'We were numb. Women hugging packets of food to ourselves and looking away as we passed each other for fear of having to share.

'Hunger was bad, the blitz was bad, but there was one bigger fear. The Russians were coming. How we longed for the Americans and British to march past our houses first.

But when their bombing paused its echoes carried on. Away to the east the Russian guns were pounding. Some ruins crumbled and fell just from the noise. I couldn't stand that noise, I couldn't stand that threat. I left my house and walked towards those guns. Old men, children, women, we all headed that way and picked up pieces of rubble to build them into a wall.

'It's funny, isn't it? Now the Russians have built a wall across the city, but we built one first. Maybe we gave them the idea. Only their wall is stronger. Ours was knocked into the trenches by the very first tanks.

'We women stopped them for a while, though. I hid in a cellar. There were seven of us. It was too many. The men smelt us out at once. They crowded the cellar steps waiting to have their turn. I don't remember how many there were, only the first. We were forced to lie down at gunpoint and he set to work. It was brief. Painful and brief. He pulled himself out after just a few lunges and looked down at his penis. It was red. He seemed pleased rather than angry, and turned to show it to the others before tucking it away. I was the most popular choice after that. There was a stone on the cellar floor that was cutting into my back, I've still got the scar, but I didn't move.'

Gran apparently made a move towards her.

'No, Vera. Stay where you are. I don't want your pity. That's not why I'm telling you this. The reason for the story hasn't even begun yet. Just sit still and listen, please. I won't be much longer.

'I don't know how long I stayed there after they'd gone. I expected to die. I suppose someone had to live. When I stumbled out of the cellar the Red Army were in the street in force. There was a lorry parked right outside my building. A woman with her hair tied in bunches and a cap with a Red Army badge squatted behind the tailboard and passed packets of biscuits to the outstretched waves of hands. She pressed a packet into my fingers and I carried it home.

'That first rape astonished me. The sight of my blood astonished me. I couldn't believe I could still bleed. I think it's what pulled me through. It let me fall in love with myself. I could look at my body and wonder how something so natural had survived. As I limped home, clutching my packet of biscuits, a flood of gratitude washed through me. Not that I was pleased to be alive in all that stink and squalor and death and ruin. Oh no. I was just deeply, deeply thankful for my biscuits.

'You must know the feeling, Vera. You've had a baby. When Tomas was born, when they handed my baby to me, I thought I would have to die, the emotion was so strong. That's the feeling.'

Mum rested a moment before finishing her story.

'One miracle leads to another. The biscuits led to Tomas. They made me start to recover, and to recover enough to seek a job when the English came to the city. Poor Douglas though, he was blind to miracles. You know his story. It's more shocking than mine. He saw those horrors on the way to Berlin that were already more than he could bear.

He couldn't sink low enough after that. You have to hit the bottom before you know if you can bounce, but Douglas could always find someone worse off than himself. He never stopped wanting to fall a little further. He would come back to my narrow bed in Berlin and lie with his arm about me till I knew he had cramp, but I didn't move. I wanted him to think of himself for once, to forget my story about those Russian soldiers, to throw aside his crippling sympathy and shake me awake. He was so bloody gentle, so considerate. It was me who had to coax him to sex, ever so gently and over the years. God knows how much of a miracle Tomas truly was. And no, I don't think your pretty English wife could have helped him. He needed someone like me, some fellow sufferer. Douglas wasn't interested in making people happy. He longed to be a saint. It's a silly ambition. You can't atone for the world. The best you can do is agree to live in it. But that was never Douglas's way.'

There was a silence, till Mum broke it.

'I'm sorry about that, Vera. Sorry, Eric. I thought I had something to say. It shows how wrong you can be. Thank you for letting us watch the television. It was a good game. Germany can win next time perhaps.'

'They played well,' Grandpa agreed. 'You've got a good team there.'

'They'll get better. Look, the sun's still shining. Shall I draw the curtains back for you?'

The curtains were pulled along the track and the room filled with light. I had relaced my boot and was tying it up.

'It's a lovely afternoon. I think I'll go for a walk. No, stay where you are. Don't see me out. Thank you again. Bye.'

The exit was too quick. I had only just tied the bow on my second boot when Mum stepped into the hallway.

'The bootlace broke,' I explained.

From the shock in Mum's face she could have just found me hanging from it.

'I've got to run now. They'll be waiting for me.'

And I did run, through the door and past the playing fields where my friends' football game had started, on past the houses and slower up the hill till I stopped to rest at the point where the car had pulled in on the day of Dad's funeral.

I stopped to think while writing this whether Mum's story had sent me running in the direction of the East, but it wasn't so. The road I took led due north out of the town. A life may be full of movement, but little of it ever in the right direction.

Interlude
ENGLAND 1975

Eleven

When my missing teeth grew back they grew at an angle. Dorothy found it funny. She laughed at my teeth and re-christened me Buck. I retaliated and renamed her Doe, after her large eyes.

For a couple of years we went around as Buck and Doe.

A system of wires and braces pulled my teeth into shape. My name got lost in childhood. Dorothy's eyes simply grew larger as life gave them more to take in.

Doe she was, if only for me, and Doe, for me, she remains. We walked each day to different schools, but met to play in the evenings.

Mark had surprised us all by leaving school at the first chance he could, a few days after his sixteenth birthday, and taking a job in a bank. Several of us had opened meagre accounts at his branch just for the excuse of viewing him in his trim haircut sitting behind a screen and totting up figures.

'I like money,' he explained.

He earned money. We stayed schoolkids. He was becoming a different breed.

Then the day came when we would go to school no more. We were passing out into the world. Doe would be leaving home for college in a couple of months. More immediately, we had a mission to accomplish.

Together with Mark we walked to a pub in town to get drunk. We sat on padded stools around a low table and downed pints of bitter till time was called and we had to leave. Already the world was different. Simply getting to our feet was an adventure. We swayed against each other and practised walking.

The town park was closed but several railings had been pulled wide enough apart for us to squeeze through. It wasn't particularly a short-cut home, but there was a good choice of bushes for Doe and trees for us and a lot of beer to get rid of. We prattled nonsense to try and rouse the birds in their cages, squawked love-calls to seduce ducks across the pond from their miniature island, and danced *Me and My Shadow* in the moonlight between the trees.

The carillon cast the longest shadow of all. The dark shape of its tower folded itself over the main park gates while the silhouette of its canopied roof was lost among the buildings of the town. I had climbed inside it several times, up past the windowed room where the carillonist would sit and smash down the levers that set the bells ringing a tune. A simple wooden staircase then led through the bell tower to a plat-form, where views around the town stretched to the hills beyond. On the way down I always stopped at the small war museum. Its display was haphazard: a collection of German banknotes mounted on walls in picture frames alongside rifles and rusted sabres, helmets and ration cards and cartridge cases and newspapers locked inside glass showcases, with a special case holding the book of the dead. A page was turned each day to bring the name of some dead soldier briefly to light.

The names of the town's dead of both wars were inscribed on metal plates fitted around the base of the tower. Doe, Mark and I rested our backs on the wall below them and slid to the ground, Doe's head resting against Mark's and my linked arms. Softly we sang a wartime medley. Pack Up Your Troubles in Your Old Kit Bag, It's a Long Way to Tipperary, on and on as each took the lead into a new song, humming when the words were lost but always hushed like it was a long lullaby to the dead.

Doe could see little without her glasses. At night she always left them behind, stepping out through the dark in a perpetual haze. We subsided into silence for a while before she spoke.

'You're really doing it then? You're leaving me?'

I was taking a train to Berlin the following day.

'Are you just going to walk out on me? After all these years?'

She was playing the baby girl.

'Don't I even get a goodbye kiss?'

She wheeled herself around from the support of the carillon tower. Her lips were full and moist as they closed against my own. Her tongue played against my gums, between my teeth, to touch my own then lap against the roof of my mouth, one hand pressed on my shoulder blade, the other around my neck to pull me closer to her.

Then she let go and pushed herself back to study me.

'Didn't you enjoy that? Don't you like me kissing you?'

'It felt good. Where have you been practising?'

'At the fishmonger's. The fish were just as responsive as you but they couldn't give a verdict.'

'You kiss well.'

'Thank you very much.'

'Don't worry, Dorothy,' Mark said, his back still to the wall. 'Big Tom is going away tomorrow whatever you do. It's too late now. I'm staying though, Dorothy. I'll be around. You won't waste your kisses on me.'

He moved forward to pull her closer but she was yet to finish with me.

'What do you really think of me? Go on. Be honest. Do you ever look at me at all? I don't think you do. You've carried the same little image of me for the past ten years.'

I had just been thinking the same thing. She had not changed much in all that time. The same ginger curls surrounded her face, her ears were still delicate, her fingers as tiny as a doll's and there were even some freckles left on her cheeks. But she had removed those glasses. Those eyes could see too much. It frightened me to have her staring at me so fixedly. There are some eyes, often blue like hers, which need the protection of glasses. She should wear them, perhaps tinted ones like those of mediums who can stare and see the spirits.

'You're his sister,' Mark explained. 'His beautiful pet sister'

'I'm not his sister. I'm nobody's pet. I'm not a little girl. And he's not my brother. I don't need a brother.'

It was late. I was drunk. I couldn't untangle the right words or make the right moves. I had to sit and watch and learn from Mark. He eased Doe round to his side, the side away from me.

'He's still a schoolboy. You're a woman. Don't expect too much. He'll grow up. He's going away tomorrow. It will be different when he comes back. You'll see. Be patient.'

'Ten years. Isn't ten years long enough?'

'Don't cry, Dorothy. Please don't cry.'

'I love him. Why can't he see I love him?'

'I love him too. We all love Tom. Now please don't cry.'

Her shoulders were heaving out sobs as Mark pushed his hand beneath her curls and stroked her neck. As he moved in front of her he looked round at me and smiled. When I replay it I want to turn it into a grin, or at least something smug, but the smile was soft. A girl he had known for years was unfolding herself in his arms. He was sharing the moment with me.

I smiled back.

He lowered his head to kiss her neck and slid his hands down to her breasts. She eased herself back to look into his eyes. He reached up to draw his fingers across the tears on her cheeks, and kissed her lips once, as though for the taste.

Standing up, he held out his hand and drew her to her feet beside him. She stayed still as he moved off. It was curious how he could play with his hands, just a touch or a sign arranging the movements of his friends. I stood up and followed him to the edge of the paved area. He spoke softly, his back turned to Doe so she would hear nothing of his voice but a murmur.

'Don't you know how she loves you?'

I knew it, but couldn't say so.

'You don't have to play brother and sister, you know. There are other games.'

'I've got to go away.'

It wasn't an answer. It was all I could say.

He pulled me close and we wrapped our arms around each other before letting go.

'She'll miss you,' he said, looking back at Doe. 'We'll all miss you. We'll just have to look after each other till you get back, eh?'

He squeezed my shoulder and took a couple of paces back.

'Send us a postcard,' he said, and winked before turning. He held out his arm and gathered Doe into it before walking her off.

I had tried to talk Mum into travelling to Berlin with me.

'All right,' she finally agreed. 'But I'm not travelling on any train. Book me a flight. With Lufthansa. I won't fly with anyone else.'

I phoned her from the travel agent's to explain that Lufthansa did not fly to Berlin. What should I do?

'Wait.'

'But they can't do anything here. And they'll be closing in a minute. Won't any other airline do?'

'Learn to wait. There are some things that you can't hurry. I've waited for years now. I'll go on waiting.'

She hung up the phone. I walked straight round to her office. She and Emma were running the Blue Angel taxi service that specialised in employing women drivers to ferry other women about the town.

'That was a waste of time,' I complained. 'You had no intention of coming to Berlin, had you?'

'I meant what I said. I will come to Berlin, but only with Lufthansa.'

'But you knew they didn't fly there.'

'They are not allowed to fly there. Why should I choose between a British, a French or an American airline? I shan't. I shall go back to Berlin with Lufthansa, or not at all.'

'Why did you get my hopes up? Why send me running around town on a wild goose chase?'

The phone rang before she could answer. Mum took the details then moved across to the radio set to call for an appropriate driver. It still amused me to see her coping so deftly with so much machinery, this woman who would not even allow a phone in the house when I was a small child. Once the business was completed she moved her swivel chair back to face me.

'Haven't you noticed yet? I do my best not to tell you things. If you ask me a question, I answer it. That's as far as it goes.'

'Why?'

'Because I've only ever learned one thing worth telling.'

'And that is?'

'That we can only learn from our own experience. There's nothing more dead than other people's stories. You've got to live your own life, not other people's.'

The phone rang again. She dealt with it, then dialled a long number of her own. A few moments later she was speaking German. She sounded curt at first, which was her way of being nervous, but soon relaxed into a smile. The whole conversation lasted barely three minutes.

'That was your great-uncle. He's quite old. I hope he survives the shock.'

She pushed a piece of paper towards me. It was the man's name, his address in Berlin, and the phone number written in a different ink at the bottom of the page.

'It was so easy. I don't know why I didn't think of it before. I simply phoned international enquiries with his name and address and they read out his number. Imagine! Just a few turns of the dial and I can make the telephone ring in Berlin. He said you're welcome to stay. You can treat his home as your own. He'll give you my old room.'

'Just like that?'

'I took him by surprise. He couldn't refuse.'

'You haven't been in touch before?'

'Not for twenty-nine years. He didn't even know I was alive.'

Her quiet smile broadened into a grin as she realised what she had done, then a call came in from one of the radio cars. She turned on the microphone and answered the query.

She waved a hand at the radio set once she was through with it.

'A woman speaks in her car miles away and her voice travels through the air. I sit here and talk to old Berlin. I don't understand how. It's simply the way my world works. Life moves on and we all move with it. Don't ask me to go back, Tomas. The past is a time not a place. I could only drag Berlin back through the years. Maybe you can make something new of it.'

She opened her diary and made an entry.

'There. I've booked a taxi to take you to the station on Saturday. What more could a mother do?'

Part Two
GERMANY 1975

Twelve

The house had a brick porch, grand and square with a steeply pitched roof, its tiles dull red and smeared with lichen, its gutters bulging with moss. Age had rusted the doorbell into the brickwork. My knock on the door set a drama going inside the house, releasing the fierce barks of a dog, the scurrying and sliding of feet, loud shouts and muttered curses and a slammed door. I stepped back to stand on the path beside my rucksack as the bolts of the door were shot back and the door pulled open.

Frau Poppel was not the kind of woman to make an entrance. Fading from the scene was more her line. For those who claim only to dream in black and white, this is the woman of their dreams.

She was in grey, a plain grey sleeveless dress fronted with an off-white apron trimmed with lace, the grey hair of her head drawn tightly back from her face and tied in a bun. Her grey eyes were shiny (they always were) beneath the arches of full, surprisingly dark eyebrows, as though she practised with the eyeliner but did not dare use tweezers. She had ample breasts and plump arms that could have made a woman feel sturdy, but refused the opportunity.

Her legs were bare, her feet slotted into simple black shoes, while the muscles seemed to quiver in her arms. Her face was fleshy too, and alive with nerves. Waves of pleasure and alarm shimmered across the surface, as though stirred by the wind of whatever she saw.

I would have guessed her to be Polish, for her air of being battered by life. A short Polish woman of about forty-two. But she was Frau Poppel.

She held her hands clasped lightly in front of her, stepped forward to stare at me a moment, then retreated in silence into the gloom of the hall. This porch was a life-size version of a weather-house, its little wooden lady pushed out on the end of a stick when the weather is set fair. As she retires indoors, her husband takes a chance to sniff the air.

Frau Poppel stood as a shadow inside the house while her husband stepped forward.

He would later tell me a story about his visit as a young man to Rome. He had stood among the crowds before St Peter's as the Pope appeared on his balcony to address the faithful. He watched the Pope closely all the while he spoke then lowered his binoculars. All those around him, everyone in that vast crowd, were on their knees. Only Herr Poppel and the Pope were left standing.

Had the Pope survived so long, I'm sure he could have verified the story. Herr Poppel was born to be noticed.

He was old, seventy-two, but not an old man. Age had simply added lustre to the tall young man the Pope might have seen. His hair was receding but still thick and long, a wave of silver combed back and behind his ears. The ears were shell-like, shells that were vast and astonishing conches with their smooth, pink, rounded bases but carbuncled surfaces and high elfin points. He did stoop slightly at the shoulders, but more likely from a lifetime's habit of protecting his head from bumps than from old age. His head was stretched forward, eager to see what came next. The heels of his black shoes were together and the toes splayed, his grey suit and waistcoat somewhat baggy and stained but excessively smart in the heat of that day.

His arms had apparently kept growing after the rest of him had stopped for his large hands hung several inches below his sleeves. His collar was frayed but much whiter than his shirt and puckered by the tight and tiny knot in his crimson tie. His neck was long; in fact every part of him seemed long like in those trick mirrors that send thick-set men sprouting. His chin was long, his nose was long, even the skin beneath his eyes, though not grey, sagged low. The eyes themselves were a dusty blue, the blue fading at the edges to merge with the whites to make them almost infinite in size.

It seemed he had not stepped forward to look at me, merely to allow the sun to stroke his cheeks and breathe in the cloud of scents that rose from the summer wilderness of his garden. He looked to the side, to the strip of blue beyond the last house on the opposite side of the street, then stared straight up into the sky before lowering his sights to me.

'Tomas. You are Tomas. Come here. Come.'

He spoke in English. I soon learned he could switch quite purposefully between the two languages, selecting aspects of each. He kept to a German accent and intonation throughout, which helped a smooth transition between the languages but showed an English learned from books rather than conversation.

What was more striking than his accent was his voice. I had already heard him shouting at the dog so I knew the sharp anger that same voice could contain, but now it was clear rather than sharp, pitched a shade higher than you would expect, a young man's voice but more confident and insistent than my own. I walked towards him.

'Hello, Herr Poppel.'

He reached up his hands as I spoke and placed them round my throat, his thumbs pressing on my windpipe.

'Speak again!'

'Hello, Herr Poppel.'

'Good.'

He moved his hands up so their palms pressed against my cheeks and squeezed the flesh on my face forwards.

'You have a good voice, Tomas. It rings down your spine. You are young, you hesitate too much, but you are fully grown. Trust your voice. It is yours. Do not be afraid of it. And welcome.'

I was standing on the path below him. He tilted my head backwards then let go to surprise me with two kisses, one on each cheek. His lips were dry but I felt the moist tip of his tongue and the surprising rasp of his stubble against my skin.

'Mara!' he called into the house. He took hold of my arm and pulled me forward. 'Come and greet Tomas. My boy Tomas.'

Frau Poppel leaned out of the hallway and reached out a hand. I took it.

'Welcome, Tomas.'

She pulled me into the house and led me on as she spoke.

'What a long journey you've had. Such a long way. Come inside. You'll be tired. You need a wash. I'll take you to the bathroom. Then you can change out of those clothes. Are trains still so dirty? I've not been on one since they ran on steam. We never leave the city nowadays, do we, Otto? If we do, when we do, we shall fly. Otto could never trust the authorities in the East. It would be so easy for them to drag him off a train and into their land. I used to hate train journeys, those specks of coal flying into my eye all the time. You must tell me what they're like now.'

'Mara!'

Herr Poppel shouted in the voice he used for the dog. She had started to lead me up the stairs but let go of my band instantly.

'Where's the boy's bag?'

'It's outside,' I answered. 'On the path. I'll fetch it in.'

'I'm speaking to Mara! How can the boy get changed with his clothes outside? Think before you talk, woman. Bring in his bag.'

I moved to follow her downstairs but she put a hand on my chest and pushed me back then kept her hand held out as she moved away, shaking her head to make sure I did not follow. With my rucksack in her arms she returned and squeezed past me on the staircase.

'And the boy must be hungry. Prepare his food. I'll show him round.'

I watched her cross the landing having dropped off the bag and disappear through another door.

Herr Poppel walked into the hallway and adjusted his tone to a kinder one.

'You are late. We expected you sooner. Mara missed church. She goes on Sunday mornings. I allow it, it does her good, she can let go of her emotions, but today she stayed at home. Emotions are still bottled up inside her. She gets too excited. Excuse her. She can go to the evening service.'

He closed the front door and walked across the brown linoleum floor. As he was turning to join me on the stairs there was the clatter of footsteps from above, a thud on the landing, then the sight of a young girl rushing down the stairs to meet us.

'Katharina!'

Herr Poppel's shout slowed her down but did not stop her.

'Hello. You must be Tomas. I am Katharina.'

She held out her hand. I took it in mine. It was small and soft and gave back no pressure at all.

'I will not introduce you,' Herr Poppel announced.

Suddenly her hand gripped on to mine.

'You know what to do,' he snapped at her. 'You know when to appear. Now go and help your mother in the kitchen.'

'Mama doesn't need help. She doesn't like help.'

'It is not for your mother. It is for you. It is good for you to give help.'

'Papa,' she pleaded.

He raised a finger and pointed the way back upstairs. She pulled her hand from mine and walked back the way she had come. At the top of the stairs she paused and looked down at me.

'I'll see you later, Tomas,' she assured me. 'We'll be good friends.'

She looked down at her father and wrinkled up her face in apparent disgust, then skipped away. I expected him to call her back but he seemed quite calm.

'She is young. Thirteen. A young and silly girl of thirteen. She has a good heart, but we must train it. These are difficult years.'

He faced the stairs, as though about to climb them, then wheeled around.

'You have met my daughter. There is one more for you to meet.'

He pulled open a door. I had heard the dog sniffing and scrabbling at its base. Now it bounded through. It locked its legs stiff and skidded across the lino when it saw me, baring its gums and growling.

'Do you like dogs?'

I nodded.

'I said do you like dogs.'

'Yes.'

'Good. A man must like dogs. Speak to him. He has to get to know you. Hassar, this is Tomas. Tomas, Hassar. We will walk him together. Hassar, sit. Stop that stupid noise. Sit.'

He swept a hand round to cuff the dog on the side of its head. It skidded sideways to collide with Herr Poppel's legs and he took the chance to thump his fist down on the dog's rump. The animal sat, dazed and controlled.

'You have German Shepherds in your country too. The police use them. Here he is my police force. We get few new visitors. We don't encourage them. The dog helps us in that. He'll soon get used to you. He's always difficult when he needs feeding. That stupid girl's forgotten him again. He'd starve to death if I weren't here. Katharina!'

He waited in silence. When there was no response he picked up the smaller of two handbells on a table in the hall and waved it furiously in the air.

'Katharina!'

He yelled the name again and again as he rang. The girl appeared at the top of the stairs but he yelled on.

'Yes!' she finally screamed.

He stopped the ringing at once.

'Feed the dog!'

She went away and returned a few moments later with a polythene bag. Swinging it in her hand she let it go. I jumped out of the way and it landed on the hall floor behind me. Before it could slide the dog was upon it, trapping the bag between its paws then gripping it between its teeth and shaking it wildly from side to side. The bag split. A line of blood scattered from the wall and across the floor, growing thicker the more the dog fought with the bag and running in channels across the linoleum as he pulled the strips of raw meat out from inside.

'He likes his food,' Herr Poppel observed.

'Hasn't he got a bowl?'

'Why does he need a bowl?'

'It would stop the blood. It's everywhere.'

'He'll lick it up.'

I doubted it. Looking around the hallway I saw the lower parts of the walls were all stained a dull brown.

'It's good practice for him. You be glad you're not a burglar. The bag would be your arm or leg. Your skin's no stronger than that plastic. He would rip straight through it to get to the meat.'

'It doesn't take him long.'

'Has he finished already? Good boy, good boy.'

He bent down and rubbed his hand along the dog's back, reaching up to fondle him around the ear.

'Now Hassar will show you to your room. Hassar! To your room!'

The dog sprang up the stairs. I hesitated, but followed as Herr Poppel pressed close on the stairs behind me.

One of the doors of the landing was pushed open. I looked inside and saw Hassar settled on top of the narrow bed that filled almost half the room. It was covered with a shiny quilt of what looked like goatskin.

'Is he on your bed? Hassar?' Herr Poppel called before stepping into the room. The dog wagged its tail. 'I said you would be friends. Already you are sharing a bed.'

'Does the dog sleep here?'

'Usually. It's up to you. He is only an animal. He sleeps where he is told. Now you will wash yourself. That door is the bathroom.' He pointed at one door off the landing, then another. 'Through that door we shall eat. A light meal will be ready in twenty minutes. I shall see you then.'

So saying he nodded and walked off downstairs.

Thirteen

Herr and Frau Poppel were seated on a sofa facing the door. Herr Poppel leaned forward when he heard me come in.

'You are refreshed? You have changed your clothes? Give your dirty ones to Mara. She'll wash them for you.'

'I won't iron them. That's too much.'

'Not now, Mara! Don't speak of this now. It is too petty. Don't bother me with it. Come in, Tomas. Sit down.'

He waved a hand to guide me to the seat opposite them. I walked in and settled down. He smiled then turned to his wife.

'Where is Katharina? Is she outside?'

'She's in her room.'

'Damn the girl. Is she sulking? Katharina!'

I jumped in my chair at the force of his shout. Katharina's footsteps sounded on the stairs.

'You may come in and meet your cousin now, Katharina. Curtsey to him.'

She stood in the middle of the room with her back to her parents, took hold of the hem of her dress, and bobbed up and down. As she went down her nose puckered and her tongue stuck out. Once she had risen again she smiled.

'That's my girl,' Herr Poppel commended her. 'You can be a lady when you choose. So tell me, Tomas. What are your first impressions of your young cousin?'

'She seems very nice.'

Herr Poppel gusted with laughter, the air shooting out from his cheeks.

'"Very nice,"' he mimicked. 'Very nice, very nice, very nice. It's Sunday afternoon and we have an Englishman to tea. Now tell me again, Tomas. Try harder. What is your young cousin like? Describe her to me.'

'She's wearing a light blue dress with a matching head-band, although her hair's plaited. The hair's very long, a shade lighter than black. It's good that it is kept back from her face. It's a pretty face, oval, and she's got a little snub nose. She doesn't need that much lipstick perhaps.'

'Katharina! Have you put on lipstick?'

'Yes, Papa.'

It was bright red and smeared in a broad ring round her mouth.

'Where did you get it?'

'Mama.'

'Mara? You don't use lipstick!'

'1 saved it. From when I was young. Before we married. I lent it to Katharina to play with.'

'The girl's thirteen. She doesn't need to play. Katharina, go and wipe it off. But first, tell me, did you do what I said? Did you pull a face and stick out your tongue?'

'Yes.'

'Did she, Tomas? Did she do that to you?'

'Yes.'

'"Very nice,"' he mimicked again. '"She seems very nice." I told you, Katharina. I told you what the English were like. I could weep for them. They have the richest language in the world but nobody left to speak it. They're all too exhausted. Thank God Americans chose to speak English. They can strip it back and make it work again.

'"Very nice". Do you think Shakespeare ever said "very nice"? Do the English think it's sweet to lie? Katharina, wipe your face clean and fetch me my puppet from downstairs. Mara, bring in the meal. I shall keep Tomas amused. Did you study Anglo-Saxon at school, Tomas? Now there was a real language.'

He stood up and took down a book from those ranged on the shelf behind him, its spine already jutting out ready to hand, and began reciting the opening lines of *Beowulf* till Katharina returned, her mouth wiped clean and a curious model in her hand.

Herr Poppel took it from her and carried it across to the window, holding it up against the light and tweaking a string at its back. The figure was of a harlequin, its neck strung from a gallows. At each pull the legs would fly up at the knees and kick high at the toes, a dance of death suspended above the earth. Herr Poppel giggled as the toy jiggled about.

'Do you recognise him?'

I shook my head.

'I said do you recognise him!' he snapped.

'No.'

'Typical. You're an Englishman and you don't recognise one of your only real geniuses. It's Shakespeare.'

He pulled the cord again to jiggle the feet.

'Shakespeare wasn't hanged.'

'I'm not talking about the man. I'm talking about the dance.'

He concentrated as the harlequin kicked up a fresh frenzy on his gibbet, roared out one loud and dismissive laugh, then let the man hang limp as he set the gallows down on the windowsill.

'I like you English. The way you gathered in your thousands and turned your public hangings into a festival. I like your gallows. It's a much funnier machine than the guillotine. And when you did chop off heads you stuck them on poles along London Bridge. Such a wonderful sense of theatre!'

'It was a long time ago.'

'And so public-spirited. There was nothing you wouldn't do to please the masses. Why, you even built a special stage and chopped off your own king's head with an axe. What theatre could hope to match that? With all the blood, all the gore, all the deaths of kings and emperors and noblemen, Shakespeare certainly tried. If enough aristocracy could die on his stage every night I suppose there was a chance the masses might not demand the real thing. It takes desperation to produce work as great as that. A whole team of aristocrats writing to save their own necks. I have a theory. There was a playwriting factory hard at work somewhere deep in the court of Good Queen Elizabeth scribbling out the works of Shakespeare. She probably gave some help herself whenever she was passing. The whole idea of men dressed as women, women dressed as men, it was all very likely hers.'

'I don't think so. There are lots of theories. They're fun, but no one really believes them. I think Shakespeare wrote his own plays.'

'You do, do you? Well, what does it matter? It doesn't matter who wrote them. "The play's the thing", isn't that what you say? It's a shame you in England will never understand those plays. Your writers writhe in agony and you smile and think they're dancing.'

He felt for the string on his model once again and pulled it. The man came to life for a moment and kicked his heels, but the joke had died.

'Someone should translate Shakespeare for the English. You will have to go and see the plays in German, then perhaps you will understand. It will help you.'

'Help me to do what?'

'You've crossed the sea. It will help you to leave your little island behind. "To be or not to be", that's the perfect question for you English. One question that goes round and round, like an Englishman pacing his shores. Have you seen *The Tempest?*'

'I read it at school.'

'Shakespeare's last play, but just like all the others. It is about a man longing to escape from his island. Surrounded by jabbering Calibans he longs to break his magic staff, or his pencil or quill pen or whatever gives him power, and sail away.'

'Surely it was about more than that?'

'You've read your study notes. You think you know everything. You will ignore me and learn the lesson yourself but I'll tell you in any case. When a man feels imprisoned, closed in, it doesn't matter what treats you give him. He will only long to get away.'

'But England's not a prison.'

'You don't think so? Do you know *King Lear?*'

'I've seen the film.'

'Ha! Typical! But it will do. You know poor Gloucester loses his eyes, a lovely scene for the masses. What does he do then? He has himself led to the cliffs above Dover and jumps off. If he jumps off his little island and into the sea all will be well. But of course he is tricked, and who by? The heir apparent to the British throne who "pretends" to be insane. Everything about the English, but especially their own idea of themselves, keeps them trapped. What about Cordelia, who wouldn't even take a big slice of your country as a gift? She returns to your island, lies on the shore and dies, but what has she got on her face? A smile! A smile because her spirit has escaped to France. That play should be called *The Comedy of Cordelia.* Tragedy is only for those who remain.'

Frau Poppel walked into the room carrying a large tray. Herr Poppel clicked his fingers to Katharina to stir herself to help.

'We'll be with you in a minute,' he told his wife. 'I am trying to educate this little English boy. He is a hopeless case. As bad as their wartime leader.'

'You mean Churchill?'

'No, I do not mean Churchill. He got you out of the mess. I mean the little weakling who started the war in the first place. Your little Neville Chamberlain. Waving his piece of paper in the air and crying "Peace in Our Time". How can you work with someone like that, someone ready to hurl his country into war without the guts to admit it? It's like your "very nice" when my daughter plays the fool in front of you. How can we trust you? You wrap words around yourselves to feel more secure. Words aren't like that. It's like trying to wear a bearskin before you've killed and fleeced the bear.'

'Dinner's ready.'

'Wait a minute, woman. I've not finished. The boy's got to understand. Words are dangerous. They are a man's madness taking flight. Tame the words and the madness remains. A little island madness.'

'It's getting cold,' Frau Poppel asserted. 'My husband prefers the sound of his own voice to good food, Tomas, but you'll not grow fat on his words. Let him talk if he wants to. You come here and eat.'

I walked over to my dinnerplate. It was edged with mashed potato and hot sauerkraut, while two slices of tongue licked the centre of the plate, steam rising from them as though their breath were still hot.

Herr Poppel threatened me with a spoonful of sauerkraut so insistently that I accepted the extra serving, moving my plate so he could tip his spoon and let the pile drop. It soothed him.

'Good. You must eat sauerkraut. My dietary studies have taught me that. Did your father eat sauerkraut?'

'I don't think so. I've never eaten it before.'

'There. More proof. Someone with lots of sauerkraut in their diet would not have died of cancer. It's certain. Your mother is German. What's the matter with the woman? It's a good job you have come here to us. We can still save you. Mara here will save you. Mara, Mara, *meine Zigeunerin, meine Bäuerin.*'

He pulled her hand towards him and kissed her knuckles.

'My peasant woman because she's from the land. My little gypsy because she's doomed to roam the streets of this city locked away from her home beyond the Wall. Did you enjoy your dinner, Tomas?'

'Thank you. It was very good.'

'Very good. Very nice. I'm sure. When I was your age I would have eaten that plate-load down in a moment. Now my body needs a little more care. My hunger is greater than my digestion. I'll go downstairs and lie down for an hour. Then, young Tomas, you shall take me for a walk.'

Frau Poppel had stood up and Katharina was stacking empty plates into her hands, but both stopped at the announcement.

'Papa, you don't go out.'

'Otto, that's enough. You stay in your room. The boy is young. You are old. That is a fact. Don't fool yourself. Don't forget it.'

'I am going out. Tomas and I are going out. We will take Hassar. The dog runs round and round this garden like we had him imprisoned. We will take the dog for a walk.'

'Papa!'

'Otto!'

'A short walk,' he conceded. 'Tomas will guide me, won't you, Tomas?'

'Well, you make sure you let him. Just go around the block.'

'Stop worrying, woman. You go off to church. Take Katharina with you.'

'I don't like church.'

'Good. I'm glad. Go again. Learn to detest it.'

'Papa!'

'Enough. Tomas, leave the women to clear away. You go and unpack. I'll see you downstairs in one hour.'

Frau Poppel put down her pile of plates to take hold of his elbow but he shrugged her off and stood up to walk out of the room.

Fourteen

I put a slip-chain round the dog's neck and clipped on a plaited leather leash, which Herr Poppel took in his hand before walking off to the front gate. His wife and daughter stood in the porch and watched—he had forbidden them to step any further. When we were both on the pavement he stopped and took a deep breath.

'It's so much lighter out here. I think our garden is out of control. There's a green gloom throughout the house. It's as though the walls were coated with moss. Are you any good with a pair of shears, Tomas?'

'I've never tried. We only had a yard at home, and Aunt Emma liked to keep the garden for herself.'

I had given a brief outline of home over lunch, and of how the lives of Mum, Emma, Doe and myself had become intertwined.

'It's good you got away. You need strength of character to handle two houseloads of women. You're too young. You should join the army.'

'There's no national service in Britain.'

'Nor in Berlin, more's the pity. That's no excuse. You must volunteer. One look at the streets of Berlin will teach you that. They're full of young scrags with down on their upper lips drifting here to escape the military. Imagine the sort of man who would choose to live in an occupied city. They use water cannon to clean the streets of them. I'd gun them all down. If they haven't learned the skills to defend themselves, more fool them. Young layabouts and thousands of little old women they let in through cracks in the Wall, that's what Berlin has come to. Why have you come here?'

'To see for myself.'

'Good. A good answer. You can see for me too. Let's go.'

'Round the block? This way?'

'Forget those women. Let them go to church. We'll follow the sun.'

He had already handed me the dog's leash. It walked to heel as I set off, but he didn't move.

'Hey! Where are you going? Are those women still on the porch?'

'They're watching us.'

'I'm sure they are. So you can at least make a pretence of looking after me.'

'What should I do?'

'Guide me.'

'I don't know where we're going.'

'I told you. Follow the sun.'

I stepped back towards him but didn't know what to do.

'What's the matter, boy? Do you want me to call for another dog collar and leash? Have you never helped a blind man before?'

'Blind? You're not blind.'

'You English have another word for it, I suppose. What do you call a man who can't see? Dark-sighted?'

'But you can see.'

'Light and shade. It's better than nothing.'

'I'm sorry. I didn't know.'

'Ha! Who's blind? The young are blind. I'm old, my eyes have gone, and still I see more than you. What are you doing? Let go of my elbow. I've come out for your company, not to be steered round an obstacle course. What's the matter with you? Why so nervous? Here, take my hand. Now let's go.'

The dog edged in front to make room for Herr Poppel and me to walk side by side, hand in hand, as we followed the sun.

'You read to me. You read from *Beowulf.*'

'Did you know it was *Beowulf*? That could have been any book. Did you see its title?'

'No.'

'Why do I bother? It was *Beowulf.* I know its spine. I know where all my books are. I know *Beowulf* by heart. I've had a lifetime teaching languages. You can't teach a language unless you know it, unless your pulse is tuned to its rhythm. I can recite many of my books.'

'What languages did you teach?'

'English. Latin. Greek. All the dead languages.'

'Do you still teach?'

'I'm retired. They retired me a long time ago. Now I'm a student. A student of medicine. I shall become a doctor.'

'You're at university?'

'You're always surprised, Tomas. What's the matter with you? Stop asking questions. Stop talking about me. Learn to see for yourself. As we walk, tell me the scenery. And don't dawdle. You're not shuffling me round in carpet slippers. This is a walk, boy. A walk!'

I described the lime trees lining the avenue first, as a warning for him not to walk into them. Then individual houses with their gabled roofs set back in their grounds.

'I know that, boy,' he kept insisting, telling me the name of the family that owned each property. 'I know all that. I have a picture of this neighbourhood inside my head more complete than you will ever see. I am this neighbourhood. It has grown old with me. Find some details. Tell me something new. Tell me of the changes.'

When I found an overgrown garden or spotted a fallen tree he smiled. He looked pleased to hear of a greenhouse with its paintwork cracked and grey and its panes of glass smashed. When we discovered a home that was obviously abandoned, its windows boarded up, he insisted on my pushing open the gate and letting the dog off its leash.

'Won't he run away?'

'He's a Berlin dog. Where has he got to run to? Go on, Hassar!' he shouted, and laughed. His laughter cranked up the volume of his voice as he heard the dog push through what remained of the garden.

'Shit away, my son. Shit where you please! Tomas, you must do me a favour. Pick me a rose. A young red rose.'

I went and picked one from a bush that straggled up the walls of the house. Its stem was light green and without a thorn. Herr Poppel raised it to his nose, then his eye.

'Thank you, von Trotschke!' he called out, and waved the flower towards the house before slipping it into his buttonhole. 'Many thanks for the fine red rose. Come now, Tomas. We will go.'

'Who is von Trotschke?'

'Who *was* von Trotschke. That is all that matters now. Von Trotschke was a man who laughed at sauerkraut. A banker who lived in this house and took me for a fool. Now von Trotschke is gone, and I am wearing his rose. We will walk on.'

Sometimes I guided him into the road, leading Hassar away from other Alsatian dogs that flung themselves at garden fences while Hassar pulled and barked in response. Herr Poppel snatched the leash from me each time and yanked it hard to pull the dog's collar into its neck, then stood and waited for me to take his hand again and lead him to the other side of the road.

'Your Queen has corgies. What use are they? In Germany we still have real dogs.'

He smiled all the time, determined to enjoy almost everything. Only one sight got him annoyed. His face had already grown sour at the sound of young children playing in the garden. When I described the signs that builders were at work, the cement mixer and mound of sand and pallet of bricks and stack of wood waiting to complete a conservatory extension, he pulled at my hand and started walking away.

'Ridiculous people. Do they think they're too big for our houses? Why do they need their conservatory? What will they do, sit in it so we can laugh at them from the street?'

We walked on, but could not go far. I was surprised to see the road ahead was blocked, but kept on walking. When we stopped, it was Herr Poppel who explained the sight to me.

'Why have we stopped? Is this the Wall?'

'That's the Wall?'

'What did you expect? Describe it to me.'

It was low. If I had stood on his shoulders I could have looked over it. Just a crude, blank, pale concrete wall.

'I never expected it. Not here.'

'We followed the sun. We walked west. We had to hit it. That's the end of our walk.'

'We could go left. There's a path going left.'

'Next time, little Englander. Next time you and Hassar can go left. You can tell me what you find. Life's funny, yes? You leave one little island, and come straight to another.'

Fifteen

Breakfast was served without comment. Five fried eggs, the whites pure white and the yolks unbroken, coated with melted butter, were laid across four slices of toast. Frau Poppel sat opposite, her elbows on the table and her chin cupped in her hands, and watched me eat. Her face showed surprise as I set down my knife and fork on a plate still runny with yolk.

'More toast?'

I declined, and she carried the plate to the sink, returning to pour me a drink.

'I've made tea. That's what the English drink in the mornings. Sugar?'

She held the spoon poised above the sugar bowl and stared at me. How can a person's eyes be so moist all the time, as though awash with a lifetime's tears? Her eyes were a constant invitation to leap inside them and let your emotions flood with hers. The teaspoon was held ready to spoon me.

I didn't usually drink tea. I decided not to take sugar. She studied me a while before speaking.

'I don't know if we can afford to have you here.'

'It's all right. I don't eat that many eggs normally. And I'll pay rent. I'll get a job.'

'Don't be so stupid. That isn't what I meant. I am worried about my husband. He is an old man with a young man's dreams. He won't look after himself. I have to do it for him. You make him too excited.'

'I'm sorry. What have I done wrong?'

'You are here. That is all. You can do nothing about it.'

'Do you want me to leave?'

'I want you to stay. It's good for me to have you here. But maybe it can't work. It's nature's fault, not yours. You men are so competitive. You have to be best at everything. While you are here my husband will try to be younger than you. That's the way it is. You shouldn't have gone for that walk yesterday.'

'I think he enjoyed it.'

'I know he enjoyed it. For some people that is enough. For some people of seventy-two such a walk is a miracle. My husband isn't interested in miracles. He's interested in making things happen. Usually he is up with the sun. I go into his room in the mornings and he is dressed and sitting in his chair, his mind already at work. This morning I walk in and the curtains are still drawn, he is fast asleep in bed. He told me he had been dreaming. He let me help him dress. You've agitated him. You've stirred his memory.'

'Isn't that good?'

'Why is it so good? The past is past. We've already lived it. Why live it again?'

'Some of it gets forgotten otherwise.'

'What's wrong with that? I envy the power to forget. It's a virtue. What do you want my husband to do, sit and babble on about the past all day? That's typical of the young. They have their youth, they have the future, and now they want to claim the past as well. They want old folk on hand so they can wheel them out in idle moments and be amused by their tales. Well, that won't happen here. My husband is exceptional. He was exceptional when young and he is exceptional still. He applies himself. Through all these years he has applied himself. That adds up to an incredible momentum. It's carrying him forward still. The world has need of what such a man can discover. Don't stop him now. Don't turn him back on himself.'

'I don't want to stop him. I like him. He's good company.'

'He doesn't need your company. I'm sure you could become good friends. That's not important. What about me? Do you think I wouldn't enjoy some friends of my own age? I would. I would like some company. I would like to amuse away some of the hours. But it isn't to be. I know what I have to do. I have to take care of my husband, to make sure he achieves everything he can. That is enough for me. I can ask no more of life.'

'You have a friend in Jesus,' Herr Poppel announced from the doorway. He had apparently been standing and listening outside the door, and now came in. 'You should have gone to church yesterday like I told you to.'

'How could I? You were gone so long. We were worried. By the time you were back and settled in it was too late.'

'Well, go today. Go and kneel in a church somewhere and wait for a mass to start. I won't have you drifting around the house feeling pious all week. Excuse Mara, Tomas. Of course you will stay with us. And we shall go out again. We shall have some good times. My wife has forgotten what a good time is, eh, Mara? Mara, Mara, Mara?'

He moved towards the table, felt for a chair, sat down on it, and slapped his hands against his thighs.

'Mara, Mara, Mara?' he cooed.

He was smirking. His words were a love call. Frau Poppel stood up, but not to sit on his lap.

'I'll make you a drink.'

'No, I'll make it. Bring me the things.'

She brought a thick glass tumbler, a jug of milk, and a box of ten eggs to the table. He took four eggs from the box, smashed each one single-handed against the rim of the glass and pulled back the shell to let the egg fall inside.

'That's the sign of a good chef.' He licked his fingers clean. 'To be able to break an egg with only one hand.'

He had evidently tired of the show. Frau Poppel took the discarded shells to the bin and brought back a cloth to wipe the mess from the table. Using the fork and a finger she worked the pieces of broken shell out of the glass, poured in some milk, then beat the mixture together.

'Mara is not a chef. She is a cook. A good cook. You enjoyed your breakfast?'

'It was very nice, thank you.'

He laughed softly.

'It was very filling.'

'You had eggs? Of course you had eggs. Mara knows what is good for you. Have you told him the story, Mara?'

'It's your story.'

'Katharina was very weak as a child. She had to go into hospital when Hassar was a puppy. Her mother went with her, leaving me to look after the dog on my own. It was a scraggy beast. "The eggs are in the fridge," Mara said. "Give it one in the morning and one in the afternoon." I looked in the fridge. There were two packs of eggs. I gave him one pack in the morning and the other in the afternoon, then went out and bought two more for the next day. When Mara got back home she couldn't believe it. Her miserable little puppy had turned into a wolf. That's how I learned about eggs. That's not true of course. It took a lot of study for me finally to learn about eggs. But it was a practical lesson that set me on my way.'

Frau Poppel slid the glass across the table and into his hand. He tipped it back and gulped the drink down in one, his tongue sticking out to lick some of the coating from the inside of the glass as he turned it before setting it back on the table.

'Eeeuch. I still can't stand the taste of it. Mara, bring us a beer.'

'It's early morning.'

'And I want a beer. I want to share a beer with my young friend Tomas. You don't have to have one. You run along to church.'

She snapped the tops off two bottles from the fridge and handed them to us.

'You are a drinker, Tomas? Of course you are. You are English. You drink warm beer. Now we will make a little German of you. *Prosit!*'

I raised my bottle to salute his and we drank. After a mouthful I put the bottle back on the table. Herr Poppel's stayed at an angle till the last drop had poured down his throat.

'Ha! Mara! Another!'

'You have to work.' She took the empty bottle from him. 'You have to work and Tomas has to register with the police.'

'Mara?' he pleaded in a little boy's voice, his shoulders lowered and his eyebrows raised. Then he decided to save that game for another day and snapped back into an assertive mood.

'You have the dog. Tomas?'

'He sprang into my room when I opened the door. I think he's on my bed.'

'Hassar likes you. It is a good sign. Take him with you to the police station. They know the power of a dog there. They'll process your papers in moments. Then come straight back here. I have some work for you. There are some papers in my study, medical journals in English going back several years. You will read them to me. We shall study them together. I'll pay you.'

'You don't have to.'

'Just a little. Pocket money. And your board and lodging. I shall give you some money and you will give it to Mara. We must keep the women happy. You will read for just a few hours in the mornings while you settle in. It will be a happy extra for me. Usually I listen to tape recordings students at the university make for me. With the rest of your time you must get out and see the city. It's my city. I have lost sight of it. You will be my eyes.'

We took practice walks till we had reached the understanding of an old pair of lovers. It wasn't an easy process. Sometimes I would leave the dog behind so I could concentrate even harder. That was a mistake.

'Stop trying so hard.' He squeezed his hand so tight I felt the bones in my own crack. 'What's the matter with you? Why so nervous? You're like a girl on her first date.'

'Why don't you take hold of my elbow? That would be better.'

'Better for whom? Are you scared, is that it? Scared to be seen walking hand-in-hand with an old man? Scared of what people might think? Are you homosexual? Is that the problem?'

'No.'

'Then give me your hand. We'll walk together.'

My hand still hurt, but he folded it gently inside his own this time.

'Relax. I'm old, I cannot see. They are failings, but far less crippling than yours. You, Tomas, are impossibly young. Don't pretend to guide me. Don't pretend to be in control. You're not ready for that. We need each other if we're going to see this city properly.'

And off we walked, following his directions as I interpreted the view.

Sixteen

He liked to let me off the leash when there was space for me to run around. 'Off you go,' he would say, and expect me to leap off and enjoy myself.

I ran up and down Trummerberg, Berlin's only real hill. It has another more redolent name, Teufelsberg or the Devil's Mountain, as though its origins were lost in myth.

'Enjoy it, it's yours!' Herr Poppel announced. 'Your mother built it for you.'

The women of Berlin had collected together the rubble of the war and carted it to this spot, placing the stones by hand till they had created one vast three hundred foot cairn to the dead. At school we had sung a hymn, 'There is a Green Hill Far Away'. This was that hill, green and wooded and simple like the landscape of Legoland.

I ran back with reports on the white radar station and the ski slope set amongst the bushes and trees and Herr Poppel smiled, but he wasn't truly interested. He didn't need the sight describing. It was enough for him to be there, to sense the light and feel the sun and sniff the air. He was marking out his territory.

He conjured bus tickets from his waistcoat pocket whenever one was needed. No other form of getting around would do. Best of all were the double-deckers when he climbed to the top deck and sat on the front seat, turning his head to whichever view I described.

I had a map of the bus routes and was supposedly in charge, but he was reluctant to step off any bus while it still had somewhere to travel. He refused to budge and held on to our ticket as though it were a contract to sit it out till journey's end. He didn't want a tourist's version of the city, he didn't want to be directed to prime sites, he wanted simply to stretch his city to its limits. I had to sit him down in a terminus café and patiently explain the use of connections to reach the remoter parts of the city before he would consent to follow me at all.

'Don't be so smug,' he complained when I first proved it worked.

From the final bus stop I had led him up a hill along a tourist's path which passed through a rare corner of the city. It held a field of corn, running up to a strip of barbed-wire fencing that marked the beginning of the East.

'It's not a knowledge to be proud of. When I was your age I wouldn't have been seen dead on a bus. And what's so special about a field? You're supposed to be showing me the city.'

Our next bus trip took us through the neat township built up to house and amuse the British Army personnel, trim houses with neat lawns, a concrete Naafi and picture house.

'Why bring me here?' he complained. 'Why take me through your silly English gardens? Find me some real countryside.'

I tried to keep to his wish of exploring the city's outer edges. Standing on one end of Glienicke Brücke I pointed across the bridge to the Eastern side and the barrier where official exchanges of spies were made.

'I'm not interested!' He kept his head turned away. 'I live here. I'm not interested in your silly games of East and West. There's water somewhere here. Show me the water.'

I took his hand and walked him down the bank to stand below the bridge, then led him forwards to dip his fingers into the waters of the Havel. A line of buoys which played a variant to the wall was marked out in sound by the buzz of patrol boats whose wake sent waves rippling to our feet.

It gave him a new theme. He wished to go in search of water. A trip to Pfaueninsel pleased him. After a stroll around a miniature lake he sent me off to explore the dainty white tower while he lay down on the lawns and listened to the cries of the peacocks.

'They're mating,' he announced when I got back, and sat up to listen to their calls some more. 'Listen to them. They know what they're after.'

He held his head back and mimicked the call to perfection. His screech had two birds crying in immediate response, challenging the new rival.

'This was always a good place for mating.'

He sat still a while longer, then suddenly laughed.

'What's so funny?'

'Nothing you can see. It's a sight for a blind man. A mirage from my youth. The sun must be going to my head.'

'Tell me about it.'

'Never! You gather your own memories.'

The next visit was to the lake at Grunewald. It was a sight that showed me the nature of West Berlin more than any other, with its desperate will to be normal within its constrictive little space. The shore was lined with dog owners, each throwing a stick into the water while dogs hurled themselves in to retrieve them. One owner almost howled with frustration as his dog swam gaily forward but with no sense of direction, the stick bobbing far off its course. Even fallen sticks were in short supply.

I explained the scene to Herr Poppel. He had heard the shouts and splashes, now he needed time to picture the full comedy of the scene in his head. Each splash brought a laugh out of him, truly a dismissive laugh of disgust, but there were so many of them it came out as a peal of good will. I stood by the shore and saw him as others saw him, a man leaning against a tree at the edge of the wood, creased with a lunatic's laughter. I finally led him away.

'Next time we bring Hassar,' he suggested when we were settled on the bus. 'We will not feed him for a week, then we will bring him here. He won't bother with the sticks. He'll swim out there and gather all those little dogs between his teeth.'

And he laughed again, though keeping to a quiet chuckle out of unusual respect for where he was.

Our next lake was the big one. We travelled out to the packed beaches beside the Wannsee, where I spread my towel on the imported sand as he settled into a wicker deckchair, an import from the closing scene of *Death in Venice* which he shamelessly used his age and blindness to secure.

'So many people,' he mused. 'So many voices. Do clothes mute voices so much? They're laughing and crying. Are these people wearing clothes?'

They were wearing swimming costumes. I had refused to take him to the nude bathing beach, alarmed at the thought of weaving this tall old man with his silver hair between rows of naked bodies, proud in his three-piece suit with a voice so loud when he grew excited you would imagine him deaf rather than blind, demanding a detailed description of every body in sight. This Wannsee outing was a compromise. He had agreed to it on the condition that I went for a swim.

'You do your own thing,' he insisted, having decided what my own thing was to be. 'You don't want to be tethered to an old goat like me.'

But now he was growing tetchy.

'Are you changed yet? Are you out of your clothes?'

'Not yet.'

'Well, hurry up. I'm sweating here. I'll be as wet as you by the time you've finished.'

'Take off your jacket. Take off your jacket and waistcoat and shirt and vest.'

'Are you trying to shame me? Don't shame me, boy. Don't imagine you can sit there and set your body off against mine. Take off your own shirt. Go on, take it off.'

I did so.

'Now come here.'

I knelt closer to his chair. He reached out his hands to push against my stomach, run them up across my chest then take hold of my arms. He pinned them to my sides.

'Raise your arms. Go on, boy, raise those arms.'

I pushed lightly against his pressure.

'Go on, boy. Go on. Flex those tiny muscles.'

His hands rose with my arms, his fingers gripping on to my biceps.

'So you imagine that's strength, do you?'

He let go.

'You're proud to have beaten an old man? You're gripped by flab, boy. Powered by fat. There's more muscle tone in the body of a pig. When I was your age we took pride in our appearance. A healthy pride.'

'I've seen the statues.'

'What a cynical young man you are.'

'What do you mean?'

'I heard your tone. I can't see your face but I know there's a sneer right across it.'

'There's not. I—'

'Don't interrupt. Don't you dare interrupt. I'm tired of your attitude, young man. You joke about those statues.

What's wrong with them? Do you think all statues should be fashioned by feeble young men with artistic temperaments? Or do you prefer the David of Michelangelo, a sturdy young boy, with features rubbed smooth and glossy beneath an old man's fingers? At least our statues showed real men, rough-hewn if you like but powerful men with no pretence.'

'One type of man.'

'An ideal.'

'Your ideal.'

'The ideal. What's the matter with you? Is your country really so poisoned with mediocrity? What do you want us to do? Cast the common man and all the derelicts of our society in bronze and set them up on a pedestal?'

'It's better than shoving them in a gas chamber.'

'Aaaah!' He raised his finger as though striking a point in the air. 'We have come to that. You have registered your protest. Has that statement been burning your insides all this time? Do you feel better now?'

'It doesn't matter what I feel.'

'It matters. I think it matters. You feel guilty.'

'Why should I feel guilty?'

'Don't ask me. I don't know. But there's something which seems to make the young these days as miserable as hell. That can usually be put down to guilt of some sort. Me, I'm a cheerful soul.'

'If I feel guilty, surely you must too?'

'What for?'

I said nothing.

'See? You can't even bring yourself to say it. You mean the Jews? You think I should feel guilty about the Jews?'

'For everybody. For everything. Didn't you know? Didn't you know what you were doing?'

'I was a soldier.'

'But you knew.'

'About the death camps? Of course we did. We all knew something.'

'How could you carry on?'

'We were at war. We were at war before we knew. You can't stop a war. It's a machine. We were parts in that machine. When you are a part in a machine you do what you are made to do till the machine breaks down.'

'But all those lives.'

'It was wrong. Morally wrong. If it were right it would have worked. So many dead Jews should have oiled the machine beautifully. Instead the machine broke down. Case proven.'

I stood up.

'Where are you going, boy?'

I carried my bag closer to the lake, changed into my trunks, and ran into the water. The sand ran out to become sludge underfoot. Families were playing, falling off lilos, learning to swim, punching beachballs, floating among the streaks of suntan lotion that gave a skin to the surface of the water. I headed out to just beyond the line of people, pushing into the forbidden zone for swimmers where the clustered sailing dinghies were tacking carefully around each other, and struck out parallel to the shore, stretching my arms in a front crawl and letting the water surge over my head till my charge of energy was spent.

I floated on my back to face the sun, then worked a slow return breaststroke through the playing people to the spot where I had left the beach.

Herr Poppel was still in his chair, sitting erect on the padded cushion to gather as much shade as possible from the wickerwork hood. He looked alert, as though staring straight towards me. I sat on my towel and stared back, glad to have him so distant, sitting in his heavy suit, so lost and alone among the crowd of bare white bodies.

He should wear a hat, I thought. A white panama hat.

As I thought that, I wondered where my anger had gone. I was pitying him already. I could not leave him stranded on the beach for long.

I looked away while the sun dried me, across the boats and the water to an island of trees, then I stood up to return.

'I'm back.'

'You've had your swim?'

'Yes.'

'Good. It will do you good. Come here. Sit down next to me. This seat's designed for two. I'll dry you.'

'I'm dry already. I'm dressed.'

'So you want to go? What a pity. I was enjoying it here. This has been a lovely day.'

He stood up. I moved forward and gripped hold of his elbow. He flapped his arm to shake my hand loose.

'Go home, boy. Go on. Leave me. I'll make my own way.'

'But you can't. You're blind.'

'You go. I don't need you.'

I stood still.

'Are you still there?'

'Yes.'

'Why? I told you to go.'

Some of the bathers turned their heads to watch, but their interest was idle. They had not come to the lakeside for drama.

'You're still there. You think you have to stay. Well don't. Don't be so arrogant. Don't be so superior. Don't go pitying me. I don't need it. You're still dripping with your mother's milk. Don't go passing judgement on my life. Go away, boy. I forbid you to stay.'

I walked off. I walked as far as the road that bordered the beach and looked back. He was following me, shuffling his feet through the sand. As he walked he stumbled into the leg of a lone woman lying with her back to the sun. She started, rolled back, then rose to her feet to confront him.

In a moment her attitude was changed. She slipped a dress over her swimsuit, slid her feet into sandals, stuffed her towel and belongings into a beach bag, then reached for his arm to help lead him on. Meekly he let it be linked inside her own.

I walked back across the sand to take control.

'I'm sorry,' I said. 'I lost him. This beach is so crowded.'

'You should take more care.' She kept hold of his arm. 'You shouldn't bring your father here. What is there for him to do? If you want to run off and swim and play you should come on your own.'

'Well, I'm back now.'

I took hold of his other arm. He shook me off.

'What's the matter?' the woman asked him. 'Isn't this your son?'

'I'm sorry. Did I startle you?' His arm now free, he reached it round to rest it on the young woman's shoulder. Her dress had only narrow straps. His hand curved around her flesh. 'He pulled at my arm. It hurts. An old war wound. But thank you. You have been very kind. The boy can take over now. He can take my hand.'

He held the hand out for me. I had no choice but to take it. His fingers curled around mine.

'Stupid woman,' he commented when we had reached the bus stop. 'How could you be my son? With that English accent?'

He was smiling. I let go of his hand, glad that he couldn't see, glad there was no pressure to smile back.

Seventeen

Each morning the dog pushed its way into my room and leapt on to my bed as though I were not in it. It was either peculiarly skilled in handling doorknobs or had an accomplice.

I suspected Katharina. The girl had to be responsible for something. Since that first day she had effectively vanished, but like a mouse glimpsed once it was hard to believe she wasn't everywhere. She didn't play loud music as a girl her age might have done, I never heard her shouting down the stairs or her name being called out, but the patter of her feet about the house occasionally drilled its short message into the walls of whatever room I was in. It said simply *I am still here.*

The dog shifted its weight around to let me free my feet from under it and hunch my legs up close to my chest. I had not slept well, staying awake until the birds started singing and the sky grew light at three in the morning. The dog stuck his head through the curtains to stare out at the world beyond. I pulled a pillow over my head in a bid to sleep on.

'Time to get up.'

Katharina was standing beside my bed holding a cup of tea on a saucer.

'What time is it?'

'Oh, it's early. You've got to get up.'

'Why? Why do you keep letting that dog into my room? It is you, isn't it?'

'It's *his* room too. Come on, take this tea.'

I sat up and took the tea from her. She settled herself down on the chair.

'It was your mother's room too. Do you look like her?'

'A bit. I don't know.'

Sometimes I remembered my father when I looked at my own reflection. It was hard to tell.

'You look different,' I said.

Her clothes had changed. She was barefoot, in jeans and a tangerine T-shirt. The T-shirt was too small for her, which only served to show how small she still was. Her bra was strapped around her like a loose-fitting bandage. But the change in her was greater than that.

'You've cut your hair.'

'Yes. Do you like it?' The question was asked with no enthusiasm and she shook her head from side to side. The hair I had last seen long and tied back was chopped so crudely there actually seemed more of it, some hanging down in strands below her ears while thicker tufts stood at an angle to her head. 'I did it myself.'

'So I see.'

'Is it that bad?'

'Why did you do it?'

'Why not? It's only hair.'

'Is that why you've been hiding?'

'I've not been hiding. You only hide when you expect someone to look for you.'

She paused to switch to English, each word of the question prim.

'Is your tea nice?'

'Very nice.'

'I made it. Mama's cooking your breakfast. It will be ready in twenty minutes. Then she wants you out of the house.'

'For good?'

'No, stupid. For today. Father's in a mood. He needs the house to himself. It happens quite a lot. You'll get used to it. Mama's given me some money to get my hair cut properly. Will you come with me?'

'Why?'

'It's something to do. She won't let me go on my own.'

'I'll think about it.'

'Good. We'll go after breakfast.'

After breakfast I would be glad to get out.

'What did you say to him?' Frau Poppel asked.

I had dutifully cleared my plate of its eggs on toast. She slid it towards her but did not carry it to the sink as was her regular pattern. The arrested movement was oddly threatening, as though I were trapped in some domestic timewarp.

'You said something to him. What was it?'

'Nothing. I don't remember. Ask your husband.'

'He is silent. He won't say anything. He just gave me a shopping list. It's fine when he shouts. His silence is terrible. You don't know what it's like, the silence of a blind man. He turns himself inside out and all I'm left with is the mess. You said something. You said something that sent him spinning, spinning backwards into the past. What did you say? You've got to tell me. I have to know. What did you say? Did you talk about the war?'

'Only a little.'

'I knew it.'

All the while she had stared at me, unblinking, her eyes swimming, searching to be told. Now she let go of my plate and pressed her eyelids closed with the tips of her fingers, as though holding back the tears. Then she rubbed the heels of her hands into her eyes to squeeze some of the moisture out and stared at me.

'Had you planned this? Is that why you came? Had you planned this all along?'

'Planned what?'

'Don't pretend to be innocent, Tomas. Please don't do that.'

She reached across the table and took my hands lightly in hers.

'You asked questions. I'm sure you did. If you asked those questions you are no longer innocent. Tell me, tell me truly. Did somebody send you here?'

'Mum. My mother. She phoned.'

'Not her. Someone else.'

'Why should they?'

She released my hands and dropped her own to her lap.

'He trusts that dog. The dog likes you. I doubt that that is enough.'

'What am I supposed to have done?'

'You asked him about the camps. About the Jews. About the gas ovens. Don't deny it. I know you did.'

I looked back at her. She carried my plate and cutlery over to the sink, but it was too late for me to take that as my cue and leave the table. I was trapped in the conversation. She faced me again to finish it off.

'Why? What's the matter with people? You weren't even born then. What are you doing here? I had already been working for years when I was your age. You, you do nothing. You've nowhere of your own to go to. You're just crawling back into the past all the time. Well, the past isn't yours. It's nothing to do with you. If Otto can leave it all behind, why can't you?'

'We have to understand.'

'Rubbish. You can never understand, so stop wasting your time. Get on and do something of your own. How can anyone understand that war? How can anyone understand what those camps were like?'

'We can try.'

'I hear you. I hear what you say. All my life I've heard people talk about trying to understand, as though that were enough. It's not enough. It's silly, it's idle, it's wicked. Good intentions are like extra skins to such people. Dried and flaky skins that they wrap around themselves to keep warm. It's gone. That old world's dead and gone. When something dies you don't try and understand why. You grieve a little, then get on with life.'

'There are memories. Memories are part of life.'

'Whose memories? Yours?'

'Everybody's. A folk memory.'

'A story. You let yourself be troubled by a story. If you really need stories then maybe you *should* speak to my husband. He can tell you about the camps. He survived one... There. That surprised you. It surprises everyone. They call him a war criminal, they call my husband a Nazi war criminal. What a term! They forget he is also a war hero. Also a war victim. Also a man. How many things can a man be? How much can a man take? You didn't see him when they sent him back after the war. He was bones. Just his skin and bones. I was young, younger than you, and I picked him up. He fell asleep in his chair as I talked to him and I picked him up in my arms. It was easy, so easy I feared he might break, and I laid him down on his bed. See a sight like that and then you can begin to understand. You know a little more about what human life is. It's the same. We're all the same. We're nothing.'

The ending was too abrupt. It startled me.

'Don't look so shocked. You're nothing too. That's all there is to understand. People feel a horror and it pleases them. They think it's good to feel such horror. It shows their feelings for others. They are absolutely wrong. They watch that film of a bulldozer rolling a tangle of naked bodies into a pit and do you know what they imagine? They imagine they are the bulldozer. The machine has the power and they see themselves as powerful, they are shocked at what that power can do. They must stop this. Their pity is sick. They are not the bulldozer. They are just another one among those bodies. Until people accept that, they will understand nothing.'

She had clenched her hands, the fingers biting into the knuckles, and thumped this double fist against the table to emphasize her final points. I felt I had to say something, to take the charge out of the air.

'What camp was Herr Poppel in?'

'Does it matter? Does it matter what camp he was in? It was a Russian one, but it makes no difference. One camp is much like another.'

'Is that why Herr Poppel is studying medicine? So he can understand the human body?'

'I think we have talked enough. He is studying medicine because he believes he can discover a way to prolong the average man's life by at least five years. He is proving with everything he does how much could be achieved with such a length of time. I will go downstairs now and see that he is comfortable.'

'Shall I go in and see him?'

'Go out with Katharina. Walk a little, think a little. And please, go quietly.'

Eighteen

When we returned the dog Frau Poppel was standing outside the front gate, dressed in a white frock splashed with yellow petals rather than flowers, white shoes, and a white handbag strung over her arm. Her skin was white too. The dress was summery and the body was only just emerging from a long winter but she seemed determined to catch up.

'Are you ready to go? Just put the dog inside the gates.'

She marched off as soon as she spoke. I took the leash off the dog and threw it across the garden. Hassar ran to chase it and I shut the gate to close him inside before running to catch mother and daughter. We met at the bus stop as a bus swept to a halt and sucked back its doors. Frau Poppel inserted a ticket to be punched for the three of us. She settled down on a seat with Katharina while I sat in front of them, and the streets of the neighbourhood hurried by.

Ever since she found her mother waiting by the gate Katharina had been putting her questions, but they were mostly a release for her own surprise. I could see she didn't expect any answers. However, now the bus was doing Frau

Poppel's fleeing for her the woman was able to draw breath and speak a little.

'Your father wants to be alone.'

'Why? He can't be. What will he do? How will he get his dinner?'

'He's starved before. One day won't hurt him.'

'But you're always there. You get everything for him. He won't know what to do if you're not there.'

'Good.'

'Did he ask you to leave?'

'Apparently. He asked me to empty the house for him. When I went in to see him just now he got angry. He demanded to know why I was still there. He shouted at me, you know how he shouts, so I left him. I slammed his door and left him.'

'You slammed the door?'

'Yes!'

Both mother and daughter held silence for a while, then the shock of what had happened began to shake its way out of their bodies. They giggled, turned to look into each other's eyes, then burst out in a quick laugh that shook the house out of their systems and set them free for a day out. The others in the bus turned to look at them, and I did too. We were all smiling. The gathering good humour of this mother and daughter was infectious.

'I like that dress. You hardly ever wear it.'

'If I am to be forced out of my own house, I will not slink off in grey.'

'Do you think Papa will be all right?'

'He wants to be alone. We won't even trouble him with our thoughts. Forget your father. We are having a day out. Why don't you wear a dress? You looked very pretty on Sunday before that joke with the lipstick. Shall we buy you a dress?'

'Where are we going? Steglitz? Are we going to Wertheim?'

'We shall go to Wertheim, but on the Kurfürstendamm. Your father's gold card works just as well there. I am tired of rushing to the nearest shop then dashing back home again.'

Our adventure was to be an outing to a department store in the centre of the city. I couldn't share any sense of excitement.

'We'll go to their salon and see if they can do something with your hair. Why *did* you chop it about like that? You're not a boy, Katharina. We don't want you to be a boy. We're quite happy to have a beautiful daughter.'

'Why don't you come to the hairdresser's, Mama? You never have anything done with your hair.'

'I wash it. I brush it.'

'Then you tie it all away. Come on, let's undo it.'

'Not here. Not on a bus.'

Katharina laughed as she pulled away the grips. She stuck them in her pocket then burrowed her fingers into the mass of her mother's hair and fluffed it out. It billowed, falling in waves over Frau Poppel's shoulders and down her back, like the clouds of hair in a charcoal drawing. Her white face seemed tiny as it peered out through its new frame. She turned to stare into the faint reflection of herself in the window of the bus. Katharina pushed her hands up through the hair again to make the reflection turn a little wild.

'It looks lovely, Mama. Let your hair have a day out as well.'

The smile Frau Poppel turned on her daughter was nervous.

'Go on. Shake your head. Brush your hands through it. Enjoy it. It feels lovely.'

Mara Poppel's head grew playful. She swivelled it on its neck to send the hair swirling like a skirt while Katharina leaned back into the aisle to make room. Then she noticed we were approaching the Underground station and stood up.

I thought of staying on the bus. The exit was behind me, and it seemed likely that the two of them might leave without being reminded that I was there.

Frau Poppel tapped me on the head.

'Come on, Tomas. Time to get off.'

'Can't we go through the East?' Katharina suggested as we stood on the escalator descending into the U-Bahn.

'You know that's not allowed. Your father would never allow that.'

'Exactly. Let's do it.'

She could tell her mother was not yet persuaded.

'For Tomas. As a treat. Before we drag him round the shops.'

'It's not much of a treat. On a sunny day like this.'

'He can choose. You want to do it, don't you, Tomas?'

'If you like.'

'Yes or no!' she snapped. I had never seen her more like her father.

'Yes, then.'

It was like travelling through the pages of a history book that was waiting to be coloured in. The tunnels narrowed so that if you had been clinging to the outside of the train you would have been knocked off, and we passed through a run of deserted stations. Above us East Berliners were walking in the sunlight but down here all was grey, a few tattered and ancient posters peeling off the walls, a lone soldier in grey standing duty on the platform, the station signs grey with dirt and age. When the train had pushed itself out from beneath this stretch of the Eastern sector to reach back into West Berlin I stepped out on to the brightly lit platform as though released.

We took the very next train back again. Frau Poppel sat with her hands folded on her handbag, her summer dress the brightest feature in the carriage and her eyelids closed, until the doors opened and Katharina touched her shoulder to show she was travelling through the West again.

'Now I shall choose the treats,' she declared as we rose back up to street level. 'I need a drink.'

We sat with coffees at an open-air table on the Kurfürsten-damm. A giant electronic hoarding of infinite lightbulbs filled the side of a building opposite us and flashed a series of animated messages, while a stream of shoppers, tourists and businessmen pumped their legs to join the race past us along the street. It's hard to sit still in West Berlin for long. We rose to our feet to join in.

The sun was trying to scorch the city. Among the fumes of the cars people had left their scents suspended like ghosts, the perfumes and farts and sweat not so much mingling as sidling around each other, trapped close to the pavement, separate and invisible in a crowd of their own.

I was passing a stall of tourists' goods but had to stop, then call the other two back. I needed witnesses to what I had found. Small orange plastic sachets, like those containing car shampoos, were tied to a length of string. Each sachet was bulging yet empty. The emptiness was what was for sale. Inscribed in white letters across the plastic was the slogan: *Berliner Luft ist Duft.*

Berlin air is super.

'Is this real? Are they selling air?'

'Of course.' Frau Poppel was close to Wertheim and not much inclined to linger. 'It's a good souvenir. Shall I buy you one? Berlin air is special. It is free.'

She looked up the Ku'damm towards the East and frowned. I declined the gift and left the stall to follow them towards their shop. The air-conditioning beyond its doors left a chill at first, but after the initial shock it was fun to be able to breathe.

Frau Poppel shopped as though it were shocking to shop in public. She barely paused to consider what she was buying.

Goods were swept from the shelves of the toiletry department, the basket handed to an assistant to run to a central collection point and she was off, pulling several women's magazines from a rack before taking a ride up to the next floor. They were playing Abba at the record bar but she ignored the selection, her hand gliding above the tops of albums till it stopped to pluck out a record by Sweet, maybe struck by the contrast of the group's peroxide blond hair against the deep pink of the cover. Katharina offered up a couple of alternatives but her heart wasn't really in it. We moved on to the racks of jeans. Frau Poppel commandeered one of the assistants and made her daughter try on two pairs. One fitted well, the other was too large. She bought them both.

'Now we'll buy you some dresses.'

'Not here, Mama. This is your sort of shop. Buy something for yourself.'

'I'm not in the mood. Have I got everything on your father's list?'

She handed a sheet of paper to Katharina.

'Did Papa really want the Sweet?'

'The record, the jeans, the magazines, the toiletries. Nothing else? Then let's get you to the hairdresser's. You can have a perm. I'll have my daughter looking like a little girl again.'

We settled Katharina into the salon, where Frau Poppel stood herself in front of a mirror for a few minutes to pin back her hair. I was relieved to see it under control once again. In its free state the hair seemed alien to the city, almost dangerous, like a swarm of bees packed closely round her head. I was surprised at the attention it had attracted from strangers.

It would be a while before Katharina would be free to join us so we wandered off, collecting the goods then stepping through a narrow section at the rear of the shop that led to a side exit. Frau Poppel crossed the road then turned to look up at the outside wall of the store. She scanned it a while, then reached up to point.

'There!'

She was showing me a line of small dents smashed into the plasterwork.

'What is it?'

'Gunfire.'

'From the war?'

'Of course.'

She moved on, around the corner that led from the Ku'damm into Tauentzienstrasse, where we had to wait to cross the main road. Opposite us was the Europa Centre, a grand name for a shopping mall of plastic and neon. Shoppers with bags like ours stood on the other side of the road, facing us as they also waited to cross.

'It's not just the old buildings that are scarred,' Frau Poppel said. 'Look about you. The damage is everywhere. The people are scarred.'

The people looked fine to me. Various but fine.

'Look at them. Buying, buying, buying, just to cover up their wounds. Look at me in this silly old frock. What do I think I am? A happy little girl?'

The traffic stopped for us. It seemed to relieve her spirits.

'But we mustn't be miserable,' she decided as we marched into the new mall. 'Our new city has so much to offer. Look what we have for you.'

She held out her hand as though offering me the building on my right. Its walls were roughly plastered in white and overlaid with a network of dark false beams. The sign above the door offered Watney's Red Barrel if we stepped inside. It was an English pub.

'Berlin has everything,' she said.

I was glad to see that she smiled. It was a good start, but we were on a quest for her favourite joke of all.

She pressed a button and a lift rushed down twenty floors to pick us up. She paid some money to a man who sat outside the lift exit at the top, arranged to leave our bags by his table, then led me up a further flight of steel stairs.

'There!' she said.

Her voice was quiet, her hands stayed by her side. The view needed no extra gesture. Berlin was laid out before us. I recognised the sights now, the trees bulging soft and green between the buildings of the Kurfürstendamm, the long avenue leading off towards the Teufelsberg my mother had helped to build and Herr Poppel had set me to climb. Frau Poppel then took my hand and led me to the right, to see the roof of the Kongresshalle open like an oyster shell amid its thick bed of trees. Whether it's one or two Berlins, nature isn't counting. It simply waits for the time it will take over once again.

From the back of the building Frau Poppel pointed down to the solid block of the KaDeWe. 'Our Harrods,' she said, her voice tinged with a wonder that didn't sit naturally on the place.

I looked from the building back to her, and saw her face was lifted to the sphere that topped the television tower across in the Eastern sector. She noticed me watching her and her smile broadened into a grin. The sphere was silver, and spangled like one of those globes that hung above a Mecca dance floor. The sun had emblazoned a sharp white cross upon its surface.

'Isn't that wonderful?' Frau Poppel said, her voice and a gentle laugh in the following silence insisting that it was so. The cross seemed to reflect in her eyes, for they glistened more than usual. 'They are proud of themselves. They are so proud over there. They built this tower to show us in the West how smart they are, how well they are doing. Just look what God does! He paints a cross on their biggest monument!'

'It's good,' I agreed; but Frau Poppel was obviously looking for a grander response. I turned round to look at the symbol that shared the top of the Europa Centre with us, a vast copy of the emblem of Mercedes Benz. 'It's funny,' I said, but as I spoke I knew I was really out to burst her sense of fun. 'This is the sign we have in the West. A three-pronged cross in a giant ring. We have a commercial that's lit to glow through the night. In the East they have a cross that shines for free on sunny days.'

'You don't understand.' Frau Poppel's smile had dried. She turned back to the television tower. 'It's a sign. Like a rainbow. They can ignore God in the East, but He'll never forget them. They'll be saved eventually.'

She stared out above her city a while longer, then turned to lead the way back towards the stairs.

At the junction of the two main shopping streets as we stood and looked down, the island of churches had lain just beneath. Frau Poppel now walked towards it. A dark and jagged tower stood beside another of blue glass. The ruin was one of the scabs of war Berlin had chosen not to pick off itself. With its new companion church just beyond it the island was a memorial, but not to any time. The churches were new and old, light and dark, a witness to the grave and hopeful possibilities of life.

'You can wait for me out here,' Frau Poppel said, and entered the new church through its large black doors.

After a couple of minutes I followed her in. She wasn't bowed in prayer but simply sitting and looking up at the altar. I settled into a distant seat and looked around. The walls were all composed of blue glass. To enter the church was like bathing in a clear pool. I closed my eyes and let my body cool down. When I opened them again Frau Poppel was gone.

I found her outside, looking for me on the paved court-yard. When she spotted me, and saw I was coming from inside the church, she smiled.

'You went inside. Good. Did you like it?'

'I did, yes. It's so clean. So simple.'

"It's like a baptism.' She looked at the old church then turned to look again at the new. 'The death and the resurrection.'

We each had our own terms, but we shared a similar feeling.

'I come up to the city on a spree, and always end up diving in here. It eases the madness. Now I shall go home.'

'But what about Katharina?'

'You can collect her. This was meant to be your day together in any case. I've been away long enough. I want to get out of these clothes. It was silly to run away like this. There's no need for you to hurry back though. Take your time. Enjoy yourselves.'

I walked her to the U-Bahn entrance, where she took her bags and left.

Nineteen

While I was eating breakfast Katharina led her father by the hand into the kitchen. Moving behind him she pushed him gently forward so he was standing in front of me.

'He's there,' she urged him. 'Go on.'

'You've charmed my daughter.' He spoke as though I had laid a curse on her. 'You took her on the S-Bahn.'

We had used this rail system that pootled above and around Berlin as our own train set. Katharina explained her father's distrust of the network. Still administered by the authorities in East Berlin, the meagre sixty pfennig fare tinkled back into their coffers, but more alarming to those who feared the East was the prospect of these trains trundling carriages packed with East German soldiers into the heart of the city.

I suspected another motive. The romance of the system was too wild for a thirteen-year-old girl. The S-Bahn was redundant, a relic of another era. Metal notices rusted beside the tracks. They were marked by the sign of the stiff-winged black eagle and the proclamation that this was the

Reichsbahn. The stations themselves were like botanical gardens, weeds flourishing through cracks in the platform and only cut back from the rails by the wheels of passing trains.

To sit on a train was to embark on a nature trail. Tracks started on stilts for you to cast your eye over the streets, then wound tattered ribbons of green throughout the city. It was fair to imagine a generation of passengers throwing apple cores, cherry and peach stones, all manner of fruits and nuts through the open windows, and wherever they landed they would sprout. Meagre trees spindled up through the matted undergrowth, twigs strengthening themselves slowly into branches, every pale leaf something of a miracle. Stems shot flowers to splash their reds, blues, purples, yellows, whites on to the landscape, and the air in the carriage was tinted with their perfume.

We stepped from the train on to the platform and walked along it a little way. I heard Katharina say something behind me, but it was a moment longer before its sense broke through.

She was saying we had got off a stop too early.

She jumped back on to the train the moment she realised our mistake. Open-mouthed she passed me, the train's closed door between us.

'Katharina,' I shouted. 'Wait for me. I'll come to you.'

'You lost my daughter on the S-Bahn,' Herr Poppel accused me now.

'It was me who was lost.'

'It was I. If you can't even speak English correctly what is the use of having you here?'

He liked to speak English in our private talks, though might have chosen Latin if I had offered to understand.

'Now my daughter chooses to read *Wuthering Heights*. A romance of ruin and disaster.' He switched to German so that Frau Poppel and Katharina could enjoy his performance. 'What is wrong with you English? You encourage ivy to eat into your houses. You restore your churches but you never go in them. You put more care into your allotments and gardens than your homes. You take day trips to the ruins of castles and abbeys. Your greatest monument is Stonehenge. That's puzzled me, but suddenly I understand why.'

He paused to see if we could guess.

'There is no point to it! That is the point! Stonehenge has no ceilings and no walls. It is a useless building. That's why the English find it so profound. They hate buildings. They despise order. They would like the whole world to be a ruin inhabited solely by ghosts and themselves.'

Herr Poppel was not looking for a response.

'Are you enjoying the book, Katharina?' I asked.

I had suggested it when we met up at the next platform down the line, and told her something of its story. She liked the thought of herself as Catherine, her name ringing across the moors. I had learned from her how her father would often come up to her room at night to be read her bedtime story. Her room was built into the top of the house and had once been his own. Now he had learned to duck his height below its beams and bend his face to the window where as a boy he had fed night-time owls with strips of raw meat. She would describe the view to him to fix the seasonal changes in his mind, and they would often simply sit together and share the silence of the room.

'She will finish the book. I shall let her read the book but not to me. It is a young girl's book. Perhaps it will make her feel like a young girl and not a boy.'

She had countered her mother's instructions and refused a perm. Her hair was cut well but close to her head. Herr Poppel reached round for her and took her head in his hands, feeling for the sight.

'Was this a joke of yours, Tomas? To trundle my daughter around on the S-Bahn and return her to me with her head shorn like a prisoner?'

Katharina raised her hands to take hold of his and pull them off her head.

'You have forgotten, Papa. You have forgotten why you came upstairs.'

Her voice and the touch of her hands seemed to milk the anger from him.

'Where have I put it?'

'It's in your pocket. In your jacket pocket.'

He was dressed more casually than usual in a white flannel jacket.

'Go on then, Papa. Get it out. Give it to Tomas.'

He did as he was bid, bringing out a postcard which he laid face-down on the table.

Shortly after my father died an overweight boy in my class had offered me his collection of used bus tickets if I would be his friend. I knew bus tickets belonged in the small litter bins fitted at the fronts of buses, but the proposed gift was not designed to please me. Bus tickets were important to the boy.

By giving them he was creating a vacuum in his life which my friendship could then fill. I told him to keep his bus tickets but I would try to be his friend in any case. The promise was mere words.

But I took the postcard.

'I can't see it now,' he said. 'Why do I keep it? You can have it.'

I turned it over. It was a hand-coloured photograph of a gabled house sitting squarely on top of a hill. The script below it labelled the picture as Berchtesgaden.

'Is this Hitler's mountain retreat?'

'Before the war I saw it myself, from just about the point that photograph was taken. It's a fine house. You can keep it.'

'Thank you.'

'I did a lot of work yesterday. I caught up. You can read to me again this morning. Just for an hour. And we shall resume our outings. Sometimes you will have to go alone. I cannot be as free as you, but I shall manage some afternoons. And maybe an evening. I can show you Berlin by night. Berlin when the daylight goes out. That's the perfect job for a blind old man. We shall do that, yes? But now I must work.'

He felt for the hands on his watch.

'Join me at ten o'clock. Once you've walked the dog.'

He clicked his heels and bowed slightly to the room before finding his own way out.

Twenty

Herr Poppel cracked jokes like a tree surgeon might crack nuts, looking for clues to a disease.

'We have a joke in Berlin,' he announced. 'We say our mountains are just as good as those in Bavaria, only not so big.'

We were standing on the wooden observation platform in Potsdamer Platz, which gave visitors a view over the wall into the East. I had just described the hump of grass in the middle of the wilderness which marked the remains of the Führerbunker.

'Do you remember that picture on your postcard? Now you see what happens to a man when he leaves his native soil. Men seem to forget what they have to live for. They will themselves to die. What is it that drives a man to such a death? Sometimes I think I should be studying psychology, not medicine. Look at Berlin now. What is it like? A wasteland?'

The empty land spread to a line of dull concrete apartment blocks. He was right, I told him. It was a wasteland.

'Of course it is. Berlin never wanted Hitler. He never wanted to come here. And look at the country of his birth now. Look at Austria. A miserable, neutral, token country which could have been so great. The Führerbunker's become a grave. The earth always claims a man in the end. Let this sight be a lesson to you. No man can outstrip his country. If he wants to grow, he must make sure his country grows with him. Hitler went too fast. We weren't all able to follow.'

'He's got some followers now.'

Herr Poppel kept quiet, waiting to be told more.

'Rabbits. The space between the walls is teeming with them. Their burrows are everywhere.'

'It's the mines. I watched a man chase a rabbit over a field once. He ran twenty yards then exploded while the rabbit shot away. The creatures are too light to detonate the explosive. There was no point shooting at them either. The animal fell in a spot where it was dangerous to go and pick up its body, or it was cooked and blasted to fragments when a bullet struck a mine.'

The space between the walls was like a vast rabbits' playground, with the concrete blocks of tank traps set at angles to provide them with shade.

'Do you think there are this many rabbits all around the city?' I asked.

'Rabbits breed, don't they? They breed like vermin. They have us surrounded.'

'1 suppose it's like this all along the Iron Curtain. For hundreds and hundreds of miles. The biggest rabbit run in history.'

It was probably wrong to ask a blind man to imagine such a picture. I was smiling at the thought, but Herr Poppel gasped and suddenly bent low. The platform was small. I feared him staggering backwards and falling to the ground, but when I reached forward to grab hold of his arm he shook me off. He was only bending to tie his shoelaces.

Or so I thought.

He pulled the shoes off his feet and stood up. Keeping his right arm straight he wheeled it fast round then let go of the shoe to set it flying high. It was the action of throwing a grenade. If it landed on a mine it would have the same effect. He listened a moment then started the other shoe spinning.

'I'll kill them. Kill the bastards.'

He cut off his cry to listen for the landing of this second shoe. The throw was a long one. The sound was distant and slight.

'Quick, Tomas. Give me your shoes.'

He held out a hand but I was spared the need to react. His arms were grabbed from behind and pinned behind his back.

'Be careful,' I said, before he could struggle. He couldn't see that there was not enough space on the platform for a fight. The uniformed official who thought he had taken an old man under control had done no such thing. 'He's blind. My uncle's blind. Let go. Give me his hand.'

I eased Herr Poppel's arm from the official's grip and took his hand in mine.

'He's a veteran. Imprisoned by the Russians. Now he's blind. It's my fault. I shouldn't have brought him here. I didn't think. I'm sorry.'

'Bring him down,' the official ordered, but the tension was already easing from his voice. I let him do the guiding, taking Herr Poppel's hands and placing them on the rails. He went first with me behind, a pantomime of concern as Herr Poppel moved with painful care down between us, hesitating between each step, his toes first then the rest of his stockinged feet.

'Thank you,' I said, and curled Herr Poppel's hand around my elbow. He played docile and let himself be led but we were not allowed to get away so easily.

'We'll need some details. You're not from Berlin, are you? Don't you know how sensitive this place is? What's your name?'

I gave answers to a string of questions until a second official interrupted us to hold out the pair of shoes.

'And this is what you threw?'

He was speaking to Herr Poppel who kept silent throughout, leaving me to do the talking.

'It was frustration. That's all. Here you are. Put these on your feet. I'll take you home.'

'Are these my shoes? How did you get them back? I threw them over the wall.'

'Think yourself lucky, old man,' the official consoled him. 'It was a blind shot. You've saved your shoes and saved yourself a lot of trouble.'

I smiled to join in with the officials' laughter, helped Herr Poppel on with his shoes, tied his laces, and led him away.

'Did the shoes go nowhere near?' he asked when we had settled on the bus to begin the journey home.

'They were good throws, but you were standing at an angle. The second one landed nearer. It almost hit the base of the wall. Why did you do it?'

'I didn't fight a war for the sake of rabbits.'

We carried on in silence till the conductor came up to the top deck to punch our tickets.

'Another official. So many bloody officials,' he muttered once the conductor had gone. 'They're all rabbits. Every one of them.'

Twenty-one

Herr Poppel went to ground, sealing himself and his humour inside his front room. I wasn't required to read to him, and wasn't allowed to walk the dog. Hassar spent the night patrolling the gardens, and was to be left behind the following day. I was given my instructions over breakfast — to proceed at once to Potsdam.

Though Potsdam was a fairly short journey to the west of the house, I first had to travel east to the edge of the city. I took the train through beneath the wall and climbed out at one of the grey stations. A series of steps led up through chambers where passports were slid beyond blank screens and human contact was a series of numbers called through an incoherent speaker. The regulation six German marks were converted into Eastern currency and the passage through to another country unlocked.

It was a shabby process and grindingly slow, but somewhere the cogs turned and turned and time was wound backwards.

It was the only country you could literally enter through the back door. There were no rides from airports, no ships' horizons, no lines of railtrack, simply a door which led on to a side street in the capital city.

There were no signs to follow, no crowds to join, no apparent reason for being there at all. I could have found the flight of steps to lead me up to the main railway station and my next train but decided first to wander.

The first street I came to was splashed to brilliance with the bright red of bunting, flags and banners. Red is a glorious colour of revolution. It can carry messages that make the darkest of grey buildings shine with hope. Banners were scrolled down the columns of grand buildings proclaiming the thirtieth anniversary of the defeat of Fascism, even though the streets were empty of celebration.

I walked with an increasing sense of contentment. There were no crowds. There was nothing to push for. The passage along the pavement was not marked by pillars plastered with posters of events or miniature showcases that served as outposts for bright shops too full to show off all their stock in-house. There were no placards or neon lights to entice me to buy, no shop windows to arrest me as I passed, no urgency in the step of those people who were about, no strain of having to keep up. This was not West Berlin.

I followed a group of tourists into a museum to admire the remains of the Greek temple at Pergamon, transported to Berlin from a hillside in Turkey, then wandered out again. It was sunnier outside and the remains were even more impressive. When the city was sliced into its segments East Berlin seemed to have won the game. The lime trees grew along Unter den Linden, the avenues were wide, the buildings imposing. A new palace of culture had been erected, floors of orange-tinted plate glass with elevators to raise you up and lead you down, but it was an unnecessary gesture. In Alexanderplatz small children used the spurs of the television tower as a slide but the tower was not really necessary either. It was playing the West on its own terms. East Berlin could have simply kept to its old opera house and cathedral, perhaps found a brighter use for the imposing but faceless government buildings, and crowed.

The few pockets of tourists that were around grouped themselves together when their timetables promised a show. It seemed to have been put on especially to please them. A phalanx of soldiers, dressed in grey uniforms and steel helmets, goose-stepped down the centre of the widest avenue to change the guard at the war memorial. Though camera shutters snapped, colour film would have been a waste of money. The scene was a clip from black and white wartime footage. It was a strange ceremony, a brisk cartoon set to run through an otherwise sleepy city.

I paused for a beer and sausage before taking my train to Potsdam.

The ride offered me the novelty of a double-decker train. I took a seat at the top, ready to be the eyes of Herr Poppel and see a sight he would never be granted. On a hill overlooking the wall stood groups of Berliners, looking across at me as I travelled through their German countryside.

It was surprising how fast the city disappeared and the train passed through the plain of ripening wheat. From my seat I saw a haycart, pulled by a horse, a man sitting with the reins at the front while two children squatted on top. of the stack, pitchforks in hand to haul in any hay that threatened to fall. I raised my hand to wave hello but I might as well have waved to a cinema screen.

We passed the cart, then far beyond it I noticed the horizon spread out like the widest cinema screen in the world.

The wall from this new distance was tiny, a pale grey band almost like the mist that can hang low over an autumn field. It was a narrow band, a tightening belt, and behind it was a city. It was a city of a vision, the city of *Revelations* that is supposed to fall complete to earth. No other city could be so contained. It sprouted high amongst the fields, buildings surging upwards, bunched against each other as they fought for the light. The city was a growth, it mushroomed, it bulged at its seams. All around it the crops still grew, but I could have been looking through a fish-eye lens. The buildings were leaning out of the frame, eager to bite chunks from the land.

I saw West Berlin, West Berlin as a whole, while my train skirted the city. It was waiting like a gathering army intent on crossing the plain.

The street that Rousseau took into the city was renamed Leninallee. I ignored the tram to walk its length. A sign welcomed me into Socialist Potsdam. The local council celebrated itself in a slogan drawn in red flowers. The town trains rang their bells. This was a big industrial city in its own right. I had no time to see more than its eighteenth-century version.

A notice at the entrance to Sansouci Park welcomed me in the name of the collective of cafeterias. A good café can make the dullest stately home worth a visit. Sadly this looked like the dullest of cafeterias, and it was closed. Beyond it, though, acres of bright green lawn billowed out from the steps of white palaces whose paint peeled like fading skin. Some attempts at restoration were constrained to showing through the growing dilapidation. Like aged generals they commanded immense respect, but had lost their sense of vitality.

I strolled around the lawns with families who had brought their picnics and laughter and games, and children who ran to play between the trees. I wanted to run with them. I wanted to sit down to their picnics and make friends. Instead I took a train ride back past the watchers on the hill and walked through the door into the West.

Twenty-two

'Good,' Herr Poppel agreed. 'You have had a good day. And I have worked well. Now you can read to me.'

The English journals were stacked on a corner of a sideboard in his front room. The room was large but crammed with such dark wooden furniture, bookcases with glazed doors and two open gate-legged tables as well as a desk, three armchairs, and his double bed with its thick white quilt. Apart from the bed and the chairs paperwork was ranged over every surface, though the floor was cleared for Herr Poppel's passage between the furniture. Beside his armchair was a box lined with slim wooden drawers, and in each of these was stacked his collection of audio cassettes. He usually fixed a blank one into his machine whenever I read so he could play it back to himself later. I took the top volume off the highest stack of journals and began to read out the index to see what articles might suit him best.

'What are you doing?' he snapped.

'I'm sorry. You haven't got the cassette ready. Do you want me to find a blank one for you?'

'No, I do not. I've told you, I have worked well today. It's time now for some pleasure.'

He had heard me enter the house and called me in before I reached the stairs. I was carrying the evening newspaper. Though I had hoped to check with Frau Poppel first before reading it to him, I had nothing else to hand.

'Shall I read you this?'

'What? Don't taunt me. You know I can't see. Why taunt me?'

'It's the newspaper. The evening newspaper.' I hesitated but he seemed to have guessed what was coming. 'You're in it.'

'Damn them!'

'Shall I read it?'

'Throw it away.'

'There are pictures.' The story was on the inside front page. One picture showed the second shoe just leaving his hand. The other saw him standing with both shoes, acting bowed and defeated. He shut his eyes tight and turned his head, as though wincing from the sight.

'Trash. Throw it away.' He opened his eyes. 'Will you go and let that dog in?'

'In here?'

'Yes, please. I want to hold him.'

I brought Hassar in from outside. Herr Poppel reached down to pull the dog close to the side of his leg and stroke its back.

'Well, Hassar, you tried. You kept them away, but it was no use. You shouldn't have spoken, Tomas. Never speak to the press.'

'I didn't.'

'I heard you. You answered every question they asked.'

'That wasn't the press. They were officials.'

'This is Berlin. Everyone belongs to the press. Everything is a story. Did you not know that?'

He sighed.

'Ah well, never mind. Read this to me, will you?'

The envelope he held out was already slit open. I pulled out the letter, studied it for a moment, then began to read.

'Please go back and start at the beginning.'

'That was the beginning.'

'Don't be foolish. Your mother has style. She would not begin a letter like that.'

I kept silent and he explained further.

'Katharina has already read it to me. You've no need to censor it.'

'But this letter's mine.'

'How was I to know? You weren't here. Somebody had to read it to me. Now please read it again. Katharina's accent left me confused. Really you should give her some lessons.'

And so I read my letter aloud.

Dear Tomas,

We are still laughing at your letter. So my poor old uncle is blind. I'm sorry to hear that, but is he really as demented as you make out? How can he allow himself to be led about the city by you? I worry for the old man's judgement. It feels like only yesterday that I stopped having to hold your hand myself.

It was a relief to hear that you got there safely at least. So funny to see you driven away in one of our taxis! Where to, sir? Berlin! And now you're so very far away.

And will we recognise you when we see you again, stuffed full of sauerkraut and fried eggs till you're as big and wild as that mad dog? I must say I felt sick when I read about that blood in the hall—I think your aunt Emma actually was sick, but then she doesn't have a German stomach.

Otherwise we're all well. It felt a bit funny not having you around, but then life is funny. I didn't have to suffer your absence for long. You had no sooner moved out than Mark moved in! He turned up just after you left. After a row with his parents he needed somewhere to stay for a few days. Hopefully he will find a place of his own by the weekend, though I must say I quite like having him here. I hadn't realised how much you have grown up. It seems I have got used to having a man about the house. Now you're gone maybe it's time I found another one of my own!

It's strange to think of you in my old room, and walking about my city. I think of you quite a lot, then I immediately try and make myself busy. It's hard for me to imagine you there. It's good to know that you're well, but I hope you can forgive me for a strange request. Keep letting me know how you are, but don't tell me any of your stories. Not yet. Enjoy Berlin and build up some memories of your own. In a while I'm sure I'll want you to share them with me. For now I've got to get used to life without you. That's a difficult enough thing to do. I don't want you to feed me scenes from my past at the same time.

I'm writing this in Emma's kitchen. Emma and Dorothy send their love. Dorothy and Mark are off hunting for his flat at the moment and Emma's sitting in her garden. Life goes on. Dorothy I think feels rather ashamed of not coming to wave you goodbye. Even when you're not here how you make that poor girl suffer!

I've come here to cook! I'd better not put it off any longer. We miss you, but it's not put us off our food! I'm sorry I have so little to write about. Now you're a traveller you'll understand how small our world at home really is!

Have fun,
All my love,
Mum

'Did you notice the hallway when you came in?'

'No.'

'Why do you write home about it if it means so little? Go and look.'

I did so.

'It's a lot cleaner,' I reported back.

'Of course it is. Mara and Katharina have scrubbed it all day. Next week the decorators are coming in, and a team of gardeners. Why do you shame us? Why shame the poor old demented blind uncle? You are supposed to be my eyes. Tell me what you see. If you see blood on the walls, then tell me. Here. This came for you too.'

He handed across a postcard. It was a small black and white picture of the ruined Coventry Cathedral, franked on the Monday after I left. I read it to myself, then again out loud.

So you've forgotten your Gran. You forgot to say goodbye. Well, Gran's just like an old elephant. Grey and wrinkled and she never forgets. You're always in our thoughts, my love. Don't make yourself too much at home. We want you back.

Fondest love,

Gran

Her script was tiny. Grandpa had made use of the space left at the bottom to sign the card as well.

'Why didn't you say goodbye to her?'

'She didn't want me to come.'

'Is that all?'

'It's all that she could speak about. She said she'd already lost one son to Germany. She didn't want to lose her grandson as well. I decided it was best to leave quietly. I didn't want to upset her.'

'Brave words and a cowardly action. You could learn from your grandmother. I like her. She's a fighter. She never lets go.'

I tucked the postcard into the envelope from Mum as Herr Poppel felt his watch.

'Now you must hurry. Be washed and dressed as smartly as you can and back downstairs in fifteen minutes. I've booked us a taxi.'

'Where are we going?'

'You've heard from your family. Now we have to take your mind off them. This is the night out I promised you. Otto Poppel and your grandmother are in some ways the same. We never forget.'

He was already in his trousers and dress shirt. When I came back downstairs Frau Poppel was tying his bow-tie and he had put on his dinner jacket.

'You look splendid,' I said as Frau Poppel backed away to leave him on display.

'At last.' He smiled at me. 'At last you are learning to flatter. I thought you were too English, too subtle. I tell you, people can take as much flattery as you can give. Tell me, Katharina, what does my young companion look like?'

Katharina stood in the bay window with her back to the light, away from the action.

'He'll do.'

I had put on a jacket and tie and buffed some instant wax into my shoes. It was the best I could do.

'Katharina is sulking.' Herr Poppel spoke in a sing-song voice designed to needle. 'My little girl wants to go to the ball.'

'I don't see why she can't,' Frau Poppel said. 'Why can't we all go? It isn't a ball, it's a concert.'

The blast of the taxi's horn from outside handed the initiative back to Herr Poppel.

'We will have many nights. Tonight belongs to Tomas. And tonight I shall take hold of your arm. Come here.'

I stepped up to his side but he turned me round to face him. The taxi blew its horn again.

'Katharina, go and tell the taxi to wait. Does he expect me to run?'

As Katharina worked her way across the room he reached out his hands to my shoulders. My jacket was corduroy. He let his fingers run down the channels in the material.

'What colour is it?'

'Brown. Dark brown.'

He felt for the knot on my tie and rubbed the collar of my shirt between a thumb and finger, then gripped me by the shoulders again.

'Katharina was right. This is not wonderful. How old is this jacket? It's squeezing your shoulders. You've outgrown it, Tomas. It's time you learned how to dress.' He reached up to take hold of my chin. 'And how to shave. You've lacked a father. I need more time. But so be it.'

We left the house, then he took hold of my arm as we walked to the car.

Twenty-three

'Not so fast. Not so fast.' Herr Poppel reached forward and tapped the taxi driver on the back of the head. 'I am old already. Don't kill me.'

'Your daughter said to hurry or you'd miss the concert.'

'That wasn't my daughter. It was my wife.'

He settled back in the seat as the car slowed down and smiled at the driver's mistake. Katharina had not spoken a word. It was Frau Poppel who had hurried out to urge both caution and haste on the driver.

'We have plenty of time,' he confided to me. 'Mara thinks we need to collect our tickets. She knows nothing. I remember how to live.'

The Philharmonie was isolated in an expanse of wasteland, like the first showhouse in a development that was too extravagant to be copied. I was surprised when Herr Poppel started to talk me through its lay-out.

'I came with Mara on the day it opened. She described it all to me, and I've remembered it till now. It was no use my coming again with Mara. She's too honest.'

There was a long queue for returns which stretched outside the hall, where signs proclaimed the evening to be sold out. Herr Poppel ignored the news when I told him.

'Just guide me. Do as I told you. And remember, speak English.'

I led him towards the back of a foyer and the narrow steel doors of a lift. The small crowd waiting there parted to let the blind man through, but we stopped as I had been instructed and he turned to face them.

'Introduce me, Tomas.'

'This is my uncle, Otto Poppel.'

He let go of my elbow and held out his hand. It reached closest to a man who was short and stout, his girth hidden by a maroon cummerbund and a white dinner jacket cut in perfect sympathy with his body. The oil that sleeked his balding head seemed fragrant. He smiled his composure and took Herr Poppel's hand in his.

'Ivor,' he announced. 'Sir Ivor Luscombe.'

He took control and introduced Herr Poppel round his small group of two more British men with grand military titles and their refined wives. The lift pinged and we stepped inside.

'I'm so glad we made it in time.'

Herr Poppel's pronunciation of 'so' was impossibly round, more pure than an Englishman would ever dare make. The lift door opened. He indicated with his hand that the others should leave first, then took hold of the crook of my arm and we followed. The attendants in this corridor appeared well trained in deference. They didn't demand to see tickets, but were happy to study them if they were displayed. Sir Ivor showed some honest surprise when we pursued his party all the way into their private box, but recovered on the instant and helped us to a pair of seats beside the aisle.

The box was designed to hold twelve people in two rows of six. Herr Poppel smiled and played the perfect guest, smiling and nodding his head in greeting when a couple needed to pass to reach the two remaining seats. As the leader of the orchestra came out he joined in the mild applause. I found it less easy to relax, expecting a confrontation at any moment, but the conductor arrived and the music began.

It was to be an all-Mozart programme, beginning with the overture to *The Magic Flute*. Herr Poppel's smile faded with the opening chords. Each time I looked across to check how he was feeling his face seemed to be furrowed with ever sharper lines of distaste. It did not clear till the applause resounded at the close of the piece, when he stood up and took a small bow.

He smiled politely once again. This was his farewell. I stood up to guide him as he felt his way round the walls, heading for the door.

'Now show me to the lift,' he commanded once we were out in the corridor. 'We're leaving.'

'But that was only the overture.'

'When a lunatic sniggers you don't wait around for the full-blown fit. Why do they all applaud Mozart so? The little man was mad. Are they all as mad as him?'

'Didn't you like it?'

'Like it? All those tunes raging around each other? How can you like that? It's the music of a man screaming for a correct medical diagnosis. Mozart had cancer. It's undeniable. The later works all cry with the pain of it. Is it only me who sees this? When will we see these artists for what they are? When will we stop loving the sickness and look for the cure? Maybe Russia is right. Maybe we should lock all our great artists in asylums till we can learn to pity them.'

We stepped inside the lift. As we sank down the building his mood lightened.

'We did it, though. My plan worked. You English are so predictable. You're so polite it hurts.'

'How did you know they would be English?'

'This is an occupied city. They had to be here somewhere. They will always take the best for themselves.'

'Why wasn't the box full? Why weren't the seats taken?'

'When tickets are so scarce they have a value in themselves. To have a ticket is prestige enough. The best seats at these occasions are often left empty. It was a gamble, and it paid off. Two people obviously decided they had something better to do with their evening. We shall follow their example. Let's go and have fun!'

Twenty-four

They say that loss of sight sharpens a man's other senses. It is not always true. Herr Poppel sometimes seemed to take leave of his senses entirely. The taxi wound through a series of dark streets to pull up outside a small door with *Kristina's* spelt out above it in pink strip lighting. I stayed in the taxi and tried to talk him out of the venture, but he refused to listen to my descriptions. At my mention of the bow-tied bouncer at the door he climbed out on to the pavement.

Banknotes of different denominations were stored in separate pockets of his evening dress. He drew some out to attract the bouncer's help.

'Pay the driver, would you? He's to take my young companion home. Then lead me into your club.'

I climbed out to join him.

'My dear boy, make up your mind. If you're coming, come. Give me your arm. Show me the way.'

The stairs were too narrow for us to walk side by side. I went first, so I could catch him should he fall. Halfway down he reached down to grab me and hold me still, his hand closing round my neck.

'Listen!'

Down below a trumpeter was blowing the first long notes of 'Il Silenzio'.

'Now *that's* music. Do you know that sound, Tomas? It's sex so raw that it hurts.'

A note cracked as we listened.

'But it's awful. He can't play.'

'Ach, go home, Tomas. Go away. Go away and leave me here.'

'But you don't know what this place is like.'

'Exactly. I'm going to find out.'

'No, I mean it. You didn't see the photographs on the wall outside.'

'What is the matter with you?' He pushed me, not so hard that I tumbled but enough for me to lose my balance and have to race to the bottom of the stairs. He kept to his step but raised a finger to point down at me. It quivered as he spoke, his voice raised to resound above the band.

'I have let you know me, Tomas. You were a young man. You had my blood in you. It was a mistake. That blood is all dried up.'

'What have I done?'

'You treat me as nothing. As an old man. I will not allow it. There is more rage in me still than you will ever know.'

My back was to the opening that formed the cloakroom window, and my hand rested on its counter. Another hand covered mine and slid it to one side.

The hand was soft. It was empty of rings, but its pale skin was mottled with a pattern of brown freckles. The nails were long, and painted a dark blue to match the sleeveless satin gown, tightly fitting to the lady's slim figure with a neckline that cut a sharp V down towards her breasts. A chain of chunky gold links hung from beneath a purple silk scarf wound around her neck. She was looking not at me, but up the stairs at Herr Poppel.

'Otto? It has to be Otto. Otto with his grand temper.'

Herr Poppel's hand fell to his side.

'Who is that?'

He reached hold of the rail to guide him down the last few steps.

'You don't recognise me?'

'Kristina?'

'That is not too clever, Otto. My name is above the door. You have forgotten me.'

He stepped towards her window, feeling for the edge of the counter with his fingers.

'Kristina. I recognise your voice. I am blind, Kristina. Let me touch you.'

As he reached out she took hold of his hands and pressed them back down on the counter.

'Nobody touches me now, Otto.'

She turned his hands to hold them in her own, then smiled.

'Is it true, Otto? Are you blind?'

'A blind old man.'

'Then that is perfect.' She squeezed his hand. 'You do remember me, don't you?'

'Of course.'

'Then thank you.'

'For what?'

'For living so long. There is a man still living who knows me as a beauty. I was a beauty, wasn't I?'

Her head tilted a touch to the side and a lock of hair, tinted a reddish brown, floated across her forehead. Her eyes appeared to grow wider between their pencilled lines, each with an arch of spiked eyelashes worn like a coronet. Beneath the white make-up the skin was creased, feathery cracks running between the nose and mouth, and the lips painted in a bright crisp red that could have made them look clipped and austere. Instead she smiled. The lips grew full and the smile spread till it seemed to bring a natural flush to her cheeks.

'You are a beauty,' Herr Poppel assured her.

As she gazed into his eyes he must have seen something, must have caught some of the spark, her look was that strong.

'And you are as gorgeous as ever.' She patted his hand, and drew hers back. 'Who is your young friend?'

'This is Tomas, my niece's boy. Tomas, Kristina.'

We shook hands.

'He is very handsome.'

'He is English. And so very young. He needs a good woman. He needs a Kristina. Perhaps you can help?'

'Don't rush him, Otto. You were always in such a rush. He's still only a boy. You're still a boy too, Otto. Look at you. Still looking for mischief.'

'Your hands, Kristina. Give me your hands again.'

As she did so he laid them on the counter and stroked the backs of her fingers.

'Your hands are bare. Where are your rings? Kristina wore rings like a knuckle-duster, Tomas. Do you see this?'

He felt with his finger for a slender white scar on his cheek.

'The diamond flashed and Kristina struck. I see it now, Kristina. I see you on fire with your temper even now.'

He hissed a laugh between his teeth. It was a sound I hadn't heard him make before. I suddenly realised he was nervous.

'Why did you do it? I don't remember. Do you?'

'Why did we do anything? It was part of the game we played. Who knows why we played games at all. We're older now. My hands grow tired. They are better without the weight of jewels. You taught me that, Otto. After you left I learned to accept no more rings.'

'What are you doing here? Is this where we hand in our coats, buy our tickets? Are you a cloakroom attendant now, Kristina?'

'I take in coats. I sell tickets. But tonight you can go in for free. This is my place, Otto. I own it.'

'Then why…'

'Don't!' She pressed a finger on to his lips.

He took hold of her wrist and kissed the finger before moving the hand up to his nose.

'You smell the same. You have the same scent.'

She pulled her hand back. 'Don't ask questions. Go through, blind Otto, and pretend you see me in there. But go to the toilet first. The door's to your right. Can you manage on your own?'

He pushed me away when I moved to help.

'He's old,' Kristina mused when he was gone. 'We get old men in here. They have different needs, but the need to go to the toilet is often one of their strongest. I can see it in their eyes. Even in a blind man's eyes. But it's strange. Otto is old, yet the former Otto is still there. He's barely changed.'

She turned her attention to me.

'So, Tomas. Do you take after your great-uncle? Do you like the girls? We have some fine ones. I choose them myself. I still have my eye, still have my judgement. All I have lost is looks and health. I can't go through there now. Who wants an old woman hobbling round the tables or grinning from a bar stool? I have my monitors.'

She pointed to two screens which kept switching their pictures to show different scenes within the club.

'I have my pot of coffee. I have simplified my tastes. I get by.'

Herr Poppel pushed his way out of the Gents to rejoin us.

'Did you marry, Otto?' she asked him.

'I did, Kristina. Otto Poppel is a married man.' He hung his head and whined the confession, then jerked his head up to fire his next words in a burst of joke excitement. 'But we've escaped. We've played a trick. My wife thinks we're at a concert. We have very little time, Kristina, very little time. Let it be good!'

She laughed.

'So Otto Poppel was caught after all.'

'I'm a wretch, Kristina,' he admitted, then laughed along with her, his nerves forgotten. 'But Tomas is free. I'm teaching him. Giving him lessons. Through you go, Tomas. Through you go.'

A young man in a dinner jacket was standing beside the bar when we came in, listening to his walkie-talkie. He put it into his pocket and walked over to us, greeting Herr Poppel by name. We were settled at a table beside the dance floor, and our drinks order taken and supplied.

A dot of red light showed a camera fitted to steel rigging in the ceiling above us. I searched for more, and spotted three. They were swivelling through different angles to pan the room, though the lens of the one above us remained staring fixedly at our table.

'Ah!' Herr Poppel smiled when I told him, and moved his head to my directions till I told him he was looking directly into it. The smile broadened and he raised his glass to offer the camera a toast.

'Do the same, Tomas.'

I copied him.

'*Prosit!*' we voiced, and downed our drinks.

'Kristina always did enjoy devices. She was the first girl I knew to keep a telephone beside her bed. Where's the head waiter?'

I attracted him over. Herr Poppel gave a repeat order for our own drinks and asked for a bottle of champagne to be sent through to Kristina. From his waistcoat pocket he drew out a roll of banknotes and placed them in the waiter's hand.

'Do you know what you're doing?' I had seen the high denomination of the notes. 'Do you know how much you handed him just then?'

'To the pfennig. It's sad. One of the handicaps of blindness. Taking care becomes a habit. Pleasure's best when you don't count the cost.'

The band was made up of the trumpeter, a drummer and an organist. They had been playing through a selection of bored standards. In their dusky orange jackets they had stood in the half-light as the only thing to look at. Now a drum-roll built in a sense of urgency. A cymbal crashed and a spotlight pierced the darkness to light up a phone on the stage that had been set on a glass coffee table. Through speakers mounted on pillars around the room came the sound of the telephone's ringing.

'What is it? What's happening? Describe it to me, Tomas. I want to know everything.'

I hadn't expected the performance of a play. A short twist of iron stairs led from the stage up to what was apparently the dressing room door. It opened and a woman hurried out, an evening bag over her arm, flinging a spray can behind her as she pressed a final gust of lacquer into the blonde piles of her hair. She was in a panic, doing up the buttons of a silver fur coat as her heels clicked and clanged down the stairs. She rushed to the table and plucked the receiver from the phone.

The phone rang for a beat while she held it in her hand, then she spoke.

'John? Is that you?'

A man's voice crackled from the speakers. Apparently it was John. The lady's face registered intense pleasure, then alarm, the fingers of one hand tapping their long nails against the receiver while the other pressed it closer to her ear.

'Where are you, John? Are you all right? Why aren't you here?'

We learned that John would not be coming. He thought it best. Things were not as well between them as she had hoped. She was a beautiful woman, but not the one for him. He hoped she would understand, that she saw how it was better to be honest now than to share a false evening together, and he said goodbye.

I guessed his conversation was pre-recorded. He could never have stayed so cold to her passion otherwise. She breathed hot dismay into the phone. She whispered, gasped, pleaded and screamed into it. It did not much matter when he finally rang off. She was already wailing, and scarcely in need of a conversation.

Suddenly she seemed to resign herself to the loss. The receiver was left to lie on the floor as she drifted quietly around the stage. The band began to play softly to console her as she flung her evening bag to the bottom of the stairs. The coat too was hardly necessary now she was no longer going out. It slipped to her ankles and she stepped out of its nest. What use her shimmering silver evening dress? Only it was so beautiful she was reluctant to discard it at once. She teased its straps on and off her shoulders, but it was breath that held the dress as much as anything, for as she breathed out a series of sighs it slipped closer to the floor.

After I had set the opening scene for him Herr Poppel had seemed content to listen to the phone call. He frowned, his cheeks tightened, and his fingers turned his brandy glass round and round as though fully absorbed by the tragedy. However the silence that followed proved too much for him. He wanted me to fill it in, and demanded that I spoke louder as the band gained in volume. What did the woman look like? Her height, her colour, her legs, her thighs, her breasts, her eyes? I shifted my chair round and back a little so I was closer to his ear and could run a constant narrative without shouting, without having to take my eyes off the scene.

Even the lady's white satin underwear had been bought for the occasion and was no longer required. The breasts swelled from the cups of their bra, the slip and then her underpants slid down towards her shoes.

'Tell me!' Herr Poppel slapped his hand against my knee as I paused. 'Don't stop! Tell me!'

Somehow I found the flow of words for what I had never even guessed at before. There was so much flesh of an alabaster whiteness, the pad of her pubic hair was like a thick golden haze, the woman so soft and substantial and vulnerable. Sleeked of her dress, released from the confines of her costume, she was a vision of nature as intense as I had ever been allowed.

She picked up the phone.

'John?'

There was no response.

'John, John, John.'

Her cries of his name changed. Finding rhythm from the band she arched her spine and held back her head as she set the cry into a song that gasped from her open mouth. The receiver had travelled down her stomach, its cord stretched as she rubbed the earpiece between her legs.

'John,' she finally sighed.

The blast of the trumpet died away to a silence which the band respected for a moment. Then they moved into a jaunty number which brought the girl to her feet, her back straight to keep her balance on the stiletto heels as she turned to acknowledge the calls and applause from around the hall. Strangely she didn't smile. We were waiting for it, we needed it, but she didn't even stoop to pick up her discarded clothes. She simply turned and walked briskly up the staircase to be snatched from sight beyond the closing door.

'You enjoyed that,' Herr Poppel observed when he had his third brandy to hand. 'Kristina must still know how to pick her women. She never liked them skinny.'

'Are the shows always like that?'

'You're still breathless, Tomas. Here, have a drink.'

He handed me his glass.

'You should have heard yourself. You sounded like an obscene phone call.'

'I'm sorry.'

'Don't be. You made me feel older than ever before, but at least it was different. I've never heard the excitement of sex so strong in a young man's voice.'

I returned the glass to him and he took a sip before answering my earlier question.

'No, shows are not always like that. You have been treated to one of Kristina's specials. She is a special woman.'

'Did you know her well?'

'Better than I knew myself.'

'How long is it since you saw her?'

'Moments.' He fingered the scar on his cheek before continuing. 'I saw her as the phone went dead and your voice took up the story. That was a special show, Tomas. It carried a message. Kristina is a great artist, in her way.'

The next show was of a different breed. The music was upbeat from the moment of the woman's first appearance. She was dark-haired and she smiled, turning her smile like a lighthouse beam to cheer all corners of the room. She wore a long cloak striped with the colours of the rainbow, while the rest of her clothes were flung or dropped or kicked from her body with calculated abandon. The cloak was left to mask her, her arms flapping it into broad wings to reveal glimpses of her flesh as she stepped towards her audience then back to the centre of the stage, dancing the shape of a star.

The star was judged to make the approach to our table its final point. I stopped my narrative as she came closer, wary of seeming rude. She kicked one foot wide to break through the pattern then jerked herself forward, her body performing the motion of a limbo dance as the feet shifted ever nearer Herr Poppel's chair. Her thighs slid over his legs till she had straddled his lap, and the wings of her cloak spread round to encase them both as her hands linked behind his neck. In time with the thumping rhythm she closed her mouth against his lips for a kiss, stayed there for two beats, then pulled back, raising her weight to her feet and retreating with the music to the centre of the room.

I abandoned my narrative and simply watched, studying her feet first of all, the heels and toes clicking against each other as she began slowly to revolve. The band threw aside the bounce of its tune and each instrument set itself trembling as the dancer's pace increased, her elbows lifted till they were level with her neck. She gathered speed and the cloak sailed high, a rainbow balloon above which her face was a radiant blur while her naked body whirled as though it were the axis of the world.

I stood and cheered and applauded the performance as it slowed to its close. She batted her eyes and appeared to totter for a moment, adjusting herself to the stillness, then spread her cloak wide in a cheery display of herself. A slow round of curtseys was her goodbye to the room, then she stepped on to the staircase and walked away.

Herr Poppel had stood too, but not to applaud. His cheeks were moist with tears which he brushed away with a hand, but a soft smile remained.

'Come on, Tomas. It's time for us to go.'

He stopped and called to Kristina as we passed her window. She came and took his hands in hers as he held them out.

'Thank you, Kristina. It was a beautiful show.'

He raised her right hand and lowered his head to brush it with his lips.

'Are you going so soon?'

'Is it soon? You can have nothing else to show me. I have lived long enough to be forgiven. How many men can say that?'

'Few men have such need, Otto.' She squeezed his hands. 'And now you must go back to your wife. Let the boy show you to a taxi, then he can return.'

'Another day, Kristina. I've shown him the way. He's young enough to wait now. There's a big day planned for him tomorrow. He has a blind date with his cousin. He's going to Dresden.'

'Dresden!' She let go of Herr Poppel's hands and reached out to me. 'Come here and give me a kiss, young man, then bear your great-uncle away. There are only so many memories an old lady can take.'

She closed her eyes as I leaned forward.

'Oh, Otto!' Her voice had leapt a register and trilled 'He kissed me on the mouth. Go on, away, the pair of you.'

Herr Poppel giggled as she fluttered her hands to shoo us up the steps.

Twenty-five

It wasn't exactly a blind date. She spotted my Wertheim bags from a distance, probably as I stepped down from the train, and headed for me with such determination that the mass of passengers on the platform parted before her.

'Tomas.' It was not a question. She was not asking who I was. She was claiming what was hers. Stepping up on to her toes she kissed me on both cheeks then wrapped her arms around me in a hug. I still held the bags so couldn't respond.

'You must be Petra.'

'Of course I am. Who else do you know in Dresden? Let me look at you.'

She stepped back a few paces.

'Why do you dress in such dull colours? This is summer. Is fashion that drab in the West? What do you think of me?'

She raised one hand in the air, placed the other on her hip and did a pirouette.

'You've got lovely hair.' It was long, hanging below her shoulders, and shone a bright ginger. In build she was more like Frau Poppel, small but firm, though I knew the relationship was through Herr Poppel's side. She had dressed for the day in a bright yellow blouse, navy blue slacks, a white jacket and red shoes, a clash of colours that seemed to keep her permanently excited.

'Do you like it? It's the first time I've let it grow long. Everyone at school makes fun of it, but I've decided not to care.'

She bent forward to let the hair flop over her head and the curtain of it hung down to hide her face, then snapped herself back upright to fling the hair behind her.

'It's from my father's side of the family. That's why it surprises you. It's my mother who's your great-uncle's niece. What a funny way of being related. It's good, though. It means we can do whatever we like. Normally Dad would never let me come into the city on my own to meet a boy.'

'Don't you live in Dresden?'

'We're about forty kilometres away. Are those bags for me?'

'For you and your mother.'

She took the bags from me and began to lay the contents out on the platform like a market stall. The pairs of jeans, the soaps, the record, the magazines, were each brought out singly, greeted with an appreciative cry, then quietly put in its place. When she had finished she stood and surveyed the assembly of goods. For a moment I sensed her disappointment that the game was over, that there was nothing more, but she promptly sparked back into animation.

'Thank you. How clever. How did you know so exactly what we want?'

'They're not from me. They're from Herr Poppel. His wife went into the city and bought them.'

'Well, you brought them here. And you'll have to take a kiss back to your uncle Otto from me.'

The kiss this time was on my mouth. She clamped her lips to mine, sucked briefly, then pulled herself back.

'Have you got any coins?' she asked as she bent down to transfer the presents back to the bags. 'I'll put these in a locker. Then I'll show you round the city. That's what you want to do, isn't it? How long have you got?'

I told her the time of my last train. It left us almost five hours. She had been expecting far longer. As we set off from the station I wondered if she shouldn't have kept hold of the bags to weigh her down. Without them she kept throwing the occasional skipping step into her walk. It was partly exuberance, partly a way of kicking up an extra trace of speed. I had the longer legs, but she had the stamina.

We headed straight for the Zwinger Palace.

'You have to see that,' Petra assured me. 'Everybody has to see that. We've been from school three times.'

She was happy to be there again, to lead me through the splendours of the restored architecture and into rooms painted a nicotine yellow but illuminated by some of the world's greatest Old Masters. She greeted the paintings like old friends, with little time for the Rembrandts but claiming the Rubens and Tintorettos as her own. I had never thought to find humour in such paintings, but she kept taking my hand to pull me to another of her favourites. It was as though the scenes were being enacted in corners of her own pleasure garden, and if I weren't quick enough the artist's models would grow bashful and hide.

In another series of rooms strung through the cellars of the palace was a temporary display of gold, masks and plates and pitchers and ornaments set on dark blue velvet and lit to splendour. To me it all seemed pointless. Gold is made to be owned. To close it off inside glass cases for the public to see but not touch seems to rob it of its power. Petra couldn't agree. She stood subdued before each case, seemingly dazzled by the richness. She was shocked to find me bored.

'You must be spoiled in your country,' she decided. 'You have too much.'

The rooms were packed, visitors shuffling round in deep queues to admire the exhibits.

'Do you think everybody here is stupid? If you don't like these things, then you are stupid.'

'I like simple things. These are vulgar.'

'That's because you see a price tag on every piece. That's your problem. We see the hours and hours of skill and craft that were poured into that gold. We see how the metal and the man were worked together until they were one. That's what we see.'

And she marched off to see some more.

Though the Zwinger Palace was so old, restoration had left it remarkably fresh. It seemed to have sucked most of the city's former glory into itself.

There was new building everywhere but it was functional, a city built to function like a small new town. There were lines of shops, pedestrianised ways, slots for trees, benches and splashing fountains, like the first buds of a spring as a great historic city dared to grow again from out of its ruins.

The sight of the shops was enough to restore Petra's good humour.

'We must buy your uncle Otto a present,' she declared. 'He has been so good to us. What would he like?'

I remembered my thought of buying him a white panama hat.

'Perfect. I will pay for it, then you can pay me back in West German marks. That way it will be like a present from both of us.'

The logic was dubious, but she pressed the new hat on my head to help me into holiday mood then promptly bought us both lunch.

'Would Frau Poppel like a present?' she asked, having explained how effective my Western currency could be in her hands, how she could buy things for her family that were not available in any other way.

'She will enjoy seeing her husband in a hat. Can't we just walk about a little? I don't have much money left.'

She accepted with immediate good grace and led me towards the Elbe. We walked across its vast waters on a solid iron bridge.

'This is the Blue Wonder,' she explained. 'It won its name during the war. You all tried and tried, but you could never blow it up.'

Beyond the bridge was the Weisser Hirsch, a broad hill dark with trees but flecked with the colours of grand houses. We were heading for a cable car that climbed the hill towards a view.

'But don't worry. We can walk to the top and then ride down. It costs hardly anything to ride down. You can save your money.'

The road up the hill wound between summer gardens so heavy with flowers they hung over the garden walls to shadow the pavement. Blocks of private mailboxes stood beside the road to save the postman a trudge up the long and private paths. We sat in our cable car and rode back down, the sun touching the gentle colours of the city beyond the broad sweep of the river.

'Wasn't that fun!' Petra declared as we walked across the river again. 'It's beautiful up there, isn't it?'

'Who lives there?' I asked, pointing back at the splendid display of homes on the bill.

'People.'

'Which people? They're beautiful houses. Do people own them?'

'Of course.'

'I didn't think people would be allowed to. How do they manage to earn so much money?'

'They work hard.'

'I thought your system was different. It sounds like in Britain.'

'That's stupid. You're capitalists.'

'We've got a socialist government. The Labour Party. Elected by the people.'

She paused to consider the notion for a moment, then rejected it as preposterous. She wanted the conversation stopped. We couldn't know who might overhear us. We had to hurry. She wanted to visit an aunt before we left Dresden. It was a family duty. She was very old and lived alone. Whenever anyone came into the city they liked to check up on her. It was quite a walk. Did I mind?

'Not at all. Is she my aunt too?'

'Oh no. She's not even my aunt really. Just an old family friend.'

The walk became a forced march, Petra skipping beside me, but we did pause once. Below the level of our path was a large area cleared of buildings except for the black remains of the former cathedral.

'It was full when the bombs fell,' Petra explained. 'Everyone inside it died. It's left like that on purpose. So we can't forget.'

'I'm sorry.' I had been waiting to say something all day. 'I'm sorry for what we did.'

'That's war. We did the same to Coventry.'

'That wasn't the same. There were nothing like so many deaths.'

'We did it first.' She turned from the cathedral ready to resume the walk. 'Anyway, who's counting?'

It seemed as though the rebuilding programme had begun at the Zwinger and worked outwards. As we walked through the suburbs the number of houses reduced to their shells increased until in some streets every house seemed to have a ruin as its neighbour.

Petra's aunt lived on the ground floor of a building divided into flats. Petra went in first to clear the way.

'This is Tomas,' she said when she had called me forward into the hall.

The aunt studied me, her gaze passing up from my shoes through the hat in my hands to meet my eyes. Her own eyes were blue. It was astonishing to see eyes so bright in a figure so frail and grey. There were only thin wisps of hair on her head, the skin had been drawn back against the bone, but her nose was sharp and her stare direct.

Then she walked away. She had said nothing, made no acknowledgement of me at all. Petra half smiled at me in apology and showed me through the door to follow the old lady into the living room. I was settled on a stiff-backed chair beside the one narrow window in the room. The window was draped in layers of lace curtain. The theme of lace was carried around every piece of furniture-lace tablecloths, antimacassars on the backs of every chair, and mats below every ornament.

Special oblong lace mats, of a thicker material and yellow-ing with age, were set under a collection of photographs that surrounded the room. Some were in frames of embossed wood, and the more recent ones in embossed silver. It was easy to tell their ages as they were all of the same person, from his years as a baby through the achievements of schooldays to portraits of the young man in his military uniform.

'Tomas is from England,' Petra was explaining. 'He's my cousin. He's brought you this.'

She took a bar of lavender soap from her pocket, one set aside from the gifts of that morning, and presented it to her aunt. The old lady held her hands folded in her lap, refusing to take hold of it.

'I'll put it in the bathroom for you.'

The moment Petra had left the room the old lady rose to follow her. They returned a few minutes later, Petra carrying a tray that held drinks and a plate of slices of Madeira cake. She placed one of these on a smaller plate and handed it to me along with a glass of blackcurrant cordial, then settled herself on a chair between the old lady and me. Occasionally I saw those bright blue eyes peep around the girl's head to look at me, but I was obscured enough for something like normal conversation to pass between them.

'I hear you did well,' the aunt offered, to prove her memory was functioning. 'Your mother wrote to me. She told me about your essay on the nature of communism. You won something. A gold star. What does that mean? Is it good?'

'It was the top award. Twenty people won it from across the whole country. We all get to travel to Moscow.'

'Moscow! Well, isn't that wonderful.'

I was left in my corner to consider the old lady's enthusiasm for the ways of the Communist state, while the conversation worked its way around each member of Petra's family.

'And how are you, Aunty?' Petra finally asked.

The old lady mumbled something and then stood up. Her eyes glared at me before she shuffled to the sideboard and reached up with both hands to take hold of one of the silver-mounted photographs and lift it down.

'How can I be well?' she was saying. 'I'm an old lady. I survive, but I am ill. You know how ill I am. Why do you ask?'

She looked into her picture so that the eyes of the young man must have reflected her own, and as she lowered it she looked at me.

'An old woman needs a family. Gustav was my only son. My only child. If only he were here now. I would be fine then. He should be here. They killed my boy, Petra, my only boy who should be here. Where is my family?'

She put the photo back on its mat and began a slow circuit of the room, looking into each photo that she passed.

'Give me back my boy.'

Petra took hold of her aunt's arm, gave me a quick smile, and asked me to leave. I left the flat and walked along the street, as far as a ruin of red bricks marked by a sign on its iron gate as the local rectory. A tree had grown up through the pavement. I sat beneath it, closed my eyes and listened to the birdsong above my head.

'I'm sorry about that,' Petra offered when she came out to join me. 'We worry for her. She'll have to go into a home soon, I think. We can't look after her enough. We live too far away.'

'What happened to her son? Was he killed in the firebombing?'

'Before then, I think. He was fighting at the front.'

'Did we shoot him? I mean the British?'

'Maybe. I didn't think so. I thought it was the Russians. That wouldn't explain my aunt's reaction though. I'm sorry about that. I should have thought. I suppose you're the same age as her son when she last saw him. It must have brought it all back to her.'

She sat down beside me and hugged her legs tight, looking up through the branches of the tree towards the sky.

'*Please* don't let me grow that old,' she begged.

I pointed out her habit of skipping when she wished to go fast. She laughed and skipped some more.

'What time is it?' she asked as we entered the station. I told her.

'There. I told you. There's plenty of time.'

The train was due to leave in seven minutes.

'Get on now. Get a seat. That seat, there, by the window,' she instructed. She smacked me another kiss before I walked up the stairs into the carriage. 'Look out of the window. I'll be back in a minute. I've got something to show you.'

The whistle had gone when she returned. Her navy blue trousers were hanging out of one of the carrier bags. In their place she wore one of the pairs of jeans.

'Perfect!' she called, slapping her thighs. 'The others will do for Mum, but these are wonderful for me!'

I pulled down the window to call goodbye.

'You hold on to that hat!' she cried out as the train began to pull away. 'Keep it for yourself. Throw your other clothes away and keep that hat. You don't have to look so old, Tomas. It's never too late to start. Take care! Bye!'

The train gathered speed but had to turn a corner before Petra's bouncing, waving figure was lost to view.

Twenty-six

Herr Poppel wiped a finger around its inside then lifted the hat to his nose.

'You've been wearing this.'

'It's white. I didn't want my hands to make it dirty.'

'It's dirty nevertheless. Thank you, but you keep it.' He threw the hat towards me. I reached out to the side and caught it.

'Hats make my head sweat in any case. I've not studied the phenomenon, but I doubt that it's good. So you enjoyed your day? You liked Petra?'

He had seemed distracted when I spoke. I was in the middle of telling him the episode of the aunt when he interrupted with his comment on the hat. I assured him again that the day was a good one.

'You'll remember the day? You'll see her again?'

'I don't know. I'd be happy to.'

'If you would be happy to see her, then you must see her. You are ignorant of a lot of things, Tomas. That's fine, it's natural, but time is running out so let me help you. There is only one thing truly worth knowing. The future.'

'How can you know that?'

'You know it. You determine it. That's how progress is made. You have to know where you're going. You can't know what it will be like when you get there, but you can refuse to be sidetracked until you've found out.'

'How can you know where you're going?'

'You're not an idiot, Tomas. You're bright. There's no need for you ever to be lost. Go home. Sit there till you've decided what your next step has to be, then take it. You're too impatient to sit there for long.'

He handed me an envelope from his inside jacket pocket.

'This is your ticket. You fly tomorrow morning.'

'What do you mean? To England?'

'You've been discovering relatives. So have I. I've been talking with your mother.'

'Has she phoned? Today?'

'I rang her today with details of your flight. She rang me yesterday. Your grandmother's ill. She's in hospital. They want you home.'

'How ill? Is she dying?'

'We're all dying.'

'But what's wrong? Why didn't you tell me? Mum rang yesterday. Why didn't you tell me then?'

'I had made other arrangements.'

He slapped his hands against the arms of his chair in sudden irritation.

'Did you not enjoy last night? Did you want to leave Petra standing alone on an empty platform? What's the matter with you, boy? Have you no gratitude? Accept grace when you receive it.'

'But Gran's dying.'

'Don't worry about her. She's spun her life out this long. She can hold out. She's a calculating woman.'

'But you don't know her. You don't know how ill she is.'

'Don't play innocent now, Tomas. I've held her postcard. I know you fled the country without saying goodbye. I understand why. Sometimes we have to be selfish to survive. Your grandmother too is selfish. She is in pain, but she will have accepted my compromise. I granted you one more day on German soil, and she already has what she wants. She knows the time your plane is due to carry you away from here.'

I opened the envelope to check the ticket. It was a British Airways flight. Along with the ticket was a voucher from Lufthansa, a confirmation of a booking for two people on their first London-Berlin flight on some unspecified date in the future. Herr Poppel understood my silence and offered an explanation.

'I like your mother. She knows what she wants to do. I thought I would help her. The ticket is for you and for her.'

'How did you arrange it?'

'I was a teacher for many years. It was a good school. A fine platform for a professional life. I've been lucky. My pupils remember me. I have some influential contacts.'

He stood up and held out his arms. I walked into them.

'There's a taxi booked for tomorrow,' he said as he stepped back to rest his hands on my shoulders. 'Mara and Katharina will go with you. I shall stay here. Remember this room. Take faith from your mother and you will be back. I'll have tea waiting. Now where is that hat?'

I picked it up from my chair and handed it to him. He placed it on his head.

'Thank you. Thank you for the thought.'

He raised the hat from his head and held it out. I stepped forward so he could transfer it to me.

'There. I give it to you. From my head to yours. My dreams, my plans, my ideas, my sweat. Head to head. A good gift between men, don't you think?'

I stood still in the hallway after closing his door. He remained still for a while too, then I heard the creak of springs in his chair as he settled himself down, the snap of the cassette recorder as it opened, the click as it closed and the press of a button. Herr Poppel was in his headphones back at work.

'What a fabulous hat!' Katharina exclaimed.

She and her mother were both sitting on my bed with the dog between them. The picture had been composed. Katharina jumped up to destroy it.

'Let me try it on.'

The brim was held up by her ears but the hat still covered her eyes. She laughed and took it off.

'I spoke to your mother today. She sounds like a real German. I asked if I could come and stay with you in England. She said I could. Papa says first I have to learn English well but that's easy. If you can speak it I'm sure I can.'

'We're sorry to hear about your grandmother,' Frau Poppel offered. Her eyes were glossy with sympathy. 'Your case is packed. The clothes are all washed.'

'I ironed them.' Katharina held up her arm to show a burn singed on her skin. 'Look at that. I did that for you.'

'You did it because you were dreaming,' Frau Poppel said. 'You were ironing but your head was far away.'

'It was in England. Tonight I'll dream of England. But now you've got to tell me all about Dresden. What was it like? What was Petra like?'

'Not now, Katharina. Tomas has had a long day. He's got another long day tomorrow, and an early start. He needs his sleep. You too if you want to be up in time to go to the airport. He can answer all your questions then.'

They left me with the dog. He sat upright beside my bed, his stance and eyes and tail all pleading for a walk. I wasn't ready for sleep, and was still surprised by the thought of leaving Berlin. The dog leapt out of the room and down the stairs to the front door as soon as I stood up.

The sky was clear, the stars were out, the air was scented. I let Hassar off his leash to roam at will along the side roads, till we touched the wall and it was time to turn back.

The walls of the airport lounge were made of glass. Frau Poppel and Katharina stood in this window as they had promised, two miniature figures with waving hands. I waved back through my porthole, doubtful that they could see me. The timings of all the movements were precise: the taxi, the check-in, the call to board, and now the take-off. My exit from Berlin was being processed immaculately.

I buckled my belt and the plane began to roll. It gathered pace, the engine roared, and its wheels left the ground. The sensation of lift-off pressed down on my stomach as we shot into the sky. I don't have any psychic claims to lay on the feeling, but later that day I learned that this was the moment Gran died.

Well done, Gran. Perfect timing.